NOT QUITE A COUNTESS

A Georgian-set Prequel to
THE AUDACIOUS LADIES OF AUDLEY

Five squabbling guardians.
Three rivals for a title.
And one dashing cavalryman threatening to overset it all…

At fourteen, Arabella Audley inherited her father's Scottish barony—but was denied his English earldom. Shuffled between five quarrelsome guardians for six long years while Parliament dithers over naming the Earl of Audley's rightful heir, Belle's tired of being reduced to a pawn. This year, at the King's Birthday Ball, she'll finally risk a gambit of her own...

The prize? Her beloved Audley Priory, and the chance to serve its people. The plan? Broker a betrothal to one of her rivals and strengthen her claim to the earldom. A perfectly sensible strategy—until a rakishly handsome cavalry officer checkmates Belle's schemes by challenging everything she thought she ever wanted.

Caught between legacy and love, Belle must choose: follow her carefully plotted path to reclaim her inheritance, or risk it all for a love that could cost her everything. In a world where duty and desire wage war, being merely audacious may not be enough…

PRAISE FOR BLISS BENNET

"Good Lord, is this a fine romance…. romantic, funny, touching, and extremely well-researched…. perfect."—*All About Romance*, "Desert Island Keeper"

"savvy, sensual and engrossing"—*USA Today Happy Ever After*

"Bennet may be a fledgling author but her book stands stalwart with… *Devil in Spring* by Lisa Kleypas, *My American Duchess* by Eloisa James, and *A Lady's Code of Misconduct* by Meredith Duran….   I was very much taken with her assured writing, complex and unusual characterization, and verve for storytelling."—*Cogitations and Meditations*

"A refreshing change of pace from other historical romances."—*Romantically Inclined Reviews*

"This has been the year of finding incredible new voices in Historical Romance for me and I can now add Bliss Bennet to the list!"—*Passages to the Past*

"This pleasing romance… round[s] out its story with precise historical flair and genuine feelings."—*Publishers Weekly*

"Steamy historical romance with witty and memorable characters and an intriguing plot…. [W]ill keep readers turning pages from beginning to the very end."—*Night Owl Reviews*

"[Bennet's] finest achievement is the heroine who remains

unconventional to the end even when she cooperates in the most conventional of romance fiction's elements: the HEA."—*Heroes and Heartbreakers*

"effervescent. . . . a series well worth following."—*Historical Novel Society Indie Reviews*

"[Bennet has] the rare, and becoming rarer, ability to create main characters who reflect their times and are in turn uniquely, likably themselves."—*Miss Bates Reads Romance*

"A beautifully written love story that has everything you want in a great historical romance: heart-wrenching emotion, heartbreak and a great HEA… Cannot wait for the next one in the series."—*The Reading Wench*

"Catnip for the historical romance reader."—*Bookworlder*

"The human nature of the characters was genuine, even a little understated…. I cried at the end, a sure sign of emotional investment."—*Novels Alive*

"Bliss Bennet writes with flair, confidence, and style and makes the era she is writing about come to vivid life. Her characters leap off the page, the writing is crisp and the pathos, emotion, and romance is sure to keep readers turning the pages." —*Bookish Jottings*

"Bennet creates the most enticing, delightfully imperfect characters. Watching them finally achieve their happy ever after is bittersweet—you're happy they're happy, but dang it, you weren't done with them yet…"—*USA Today Happy Ever After*

Semifinalist, *Publishers Weekly Booklife Prize*
All About Romance Desert Island Keeper
All About Romance Best of the Year
USA Today Happy Ever After Must Read Romance
InD'Tale Magazine, Crowned Heart of Excellence Award
Holt Medallion, Historical Romance
Hearts Through History's *Romance Through the Ages* Award

NOT QUITE A COUNTESS

The Audacious Ladies of Audley

BLISS BENNET

FOR
ANGELIKA, GAIL, JESS,
TRICIA, AND WENDY

Critique partners without peer

THE ROYAL DRAWING ROOM

"Oh, my dear Arabella, no. Women in Scotland may flick their wrists as if they are swatting at flies, but in London a lady with any pretensions to gentility wafts her fan. Lightly, languidly, as if she has not a care in the world."

Arabella Audley, Baroness of Culmaily in her own right but not yet Countess of Audley, clutched her mother-of-pearl fan between over-warm gloved fingers. Why had none of her guardians warned her how stifling it would be in St. James's Palace, pressed so tightly against the aristocrats and courtiers and yeomen guards all waiting on the grand stairwell for the King's Birthday Drawing Room to begin?

Silly not to wave one's fan as vigorously as possible against such smotheringly humid air. Especially when no one in the crowd seemed to be paying the least attention to Belle, or to her fan.

But Lady Mowbray insisted that a twenty-year-old Scots baroness with pretensions to becoming an English countess could not afford a single social faux pas, especially during her first introduction to court.

From the stair below, Lady Kerr gave a contemptuous sniff. Offended, no doubt, on behalf of her fellow Scotswomen, as well as by Lady Mowbray's instructions on the proper way to wield a fan. Which, of course, contradicted her own.

Belle stifled a sigh. What a trial it was, being subject to the will and whims of not one, not even two or three, but *five* guardians—a Scottish duke, an English earl, two baronets (one of each nationality), and an Honorable Mr., also of the Scots persuasion. Which also meant suffering the will and whims of their ladies, too. Only three of those, thank heavens, the duke a widower and the English baronet as yet unwed. Yet each member of her Battalion of Botheration had a different opinion of how Belle should be brought up, how she should behave in public and in private, and how she could best ensure her father's second and more important title did not fall into abeyance, or, even worse, pass to a distant relation with a dubious claim.

Or whether it was even worth her while to attempt to regain her father's earldom at all.

As if Belle would ever cede her father's title, or her beloved Audley Priory, to a stranger without a fight!

A failure to plan is nothing more than a plan to fail. One of the many lessons her father had instilled as he taught his only surviving child how to manage an estate. And so Belle had devised a plan of her own to ensure his earldom would, through her, continue in his line. A plan none of her guardians would even consider. But one that would prove her father's faith in her to protect his Leicestershire estate and all its dependents, even though she was only a female, had not been misguided.

A plan that today she would finally have a chance to begin to implement.

"Baroness?" Lady Mowbray raised an eyebrow, inviting Belle to imitate the graceful turn of her wrist.

As if Belle's fan of mere horn could ever glint and glimmer in the light as Lady Mowbray's gilded mother-of-pearl one did.

Belle suppressed an uncharacteristic impulse to toss her fan, and all the illogical rules that accompanied it, right over the balustrade. Social customs existed for a purpose, her father had taught her, even the ones for which she could not see the reason.

At least none of her guardians—nor their ladies—would

bicker here, in the thick of the *bon-ton*. No, gentlemen—and even more so gentle*women*—must avoid affective outbursts, must demonstrate proper emotional regulation, if they were to ensure their social standing at the English court.

As each member of her Militia of Good Manners was all too wont to remind her.

Taking a deep breath, Belle *wafted*.

For a few moments, she allowed herself to marvel at the display of wealth and power collected at court today. The ladies flaunting the finest Chinese silks, the most intricate French and Italian brocades, the most lavish of laces from Alençon and Brussels and Valenciennes. And not just the ladies, either. The men, too, paraded and peacocked, flourishing jewel-handled dress swords and snuffboxes of silver and gold, elaborately embroidered frock coats and waistcoats, and cravats tied in ever-more intricate knots. How dear John would have laughed to see

—

Belle's fan stuttered. Her brother, her parents—none would ever come to court again.

"A pity the birthday celebrations were delayed," Lady Kerr offered. "London's dismal weather is far more tolerable in May."

"The poor king!" Lady Elizabeth Ferguson, Belle's paternal aunt, gave her arm a sympathetic squeeze. "A month is far too short a time to grieve dear Princess Louisa."

Belle swallowed, pushing down a too-familiar tightness in her chest. She had lost a brother, not a sister, as the king had. And her loss was far less recent than the king's; she'd only been ten when she'd survived an outbreak of the measles, but twelve-year-old John had not.

Why, then, did the tightness the memory of her elder brother always brought on never seem to lessen?

"We are all born destined to die," Lady Mowbray opined. "And as our monarch has already lost three other siblings before the princess, he should be resigned to grief by now."

As should she…

Belle drew in a deep breath. Time to stop wallowing in useless emotion and instead put her plan into action.

She gazed down again at the milling crowd, searching for the two men who had petitioned Parliament to be named the nineteenth Earl of Audley. She'd only met Audley Seagrave, her grandfather's distant cousin, once, when he visited Audley Priory hoping for her father's help in convincing the late king to restore his attainted baronetcy. But he'd cut a memorably imposing figure, and she thought she might still recognize him, even all these years later. She'd never caught even a glimpse of the far younger Sir Henry de Audley, but perhaps he might have inherited the noble Audley nose, or the awkward Audley eyebrows?

But even though she examined the crowd minutely, of her distant relations, she could see no sign.

Belle closed her fan and pressed it tight against the edge of her court gown's stomacher. Wrong, wrong, to feel such a flood of relief at their absence. She'd long understood she must make a marriage of alliance, not of love, if she wished to win back the Audley lands and title…

With her other hand, Belle reached inside her pocket slit, searching for the distraction of the heart-shaped silver brooch her father had given her mother upon their betrothal, the brooch that after her mother's death had passed to her. The words engraved on its back—*Before my eye, no star to thee*—stood as testament to the love that had been the impetus for their marriage.

But Belle could ill afford to indulge in idle dreams of love. Audley Priory, not romantic attachment, must be her sole object.

Her lips pressing tight, she brushed her gloved thumb against the point of the brooch's pin, a sharp reminder not to be so ill-bred as to show emotion in public. Especially not on such an important day as this.

Unwilling to see if she had drawn blood, Belle ignored her left hand altogether and focused all her energy on the other, forcing her fan to slowly *waft* once again.

A distraction of a very different sort suddenly made that hand jerk. A welcome distraction, at least, this time, in the form of a set of male shoulders standing by the entry door. *Broad* shoulders, garbed not in satin or silk but in the simple scarlet wool of an army officer. Not puffed out with padding, either, as were those of many of the courtiers waiting on the staircase. No, these shoulders were assuredly made of strong, solid muscle.

Belle's fan froze as the shoulders turned, revealing the vision of masculine comeliness to which they were attached. She blinked, then blinked again, unable to stop the color from rising in her rice-powdered cheeks. Could the eyes above those shoulders truly be fixed on her as intently as hers were caught on him?

Admiration was not the only reason a man might stare at Baroness Culmaily. But the officer was far too young to be Audley Seagrave. Might he be Sir Henry de Audley? She'd little wish to marry an elderly man to secure her father's title, although she would if she must. But if a handsome young soldier would serve equally well...

Belle frowned. None of her guardians had named de Audley a military man, had they?

Oh, merciful heavens. Had she made some inadvertent gesture with her fan, beckoning the well-thewed officer to her side? For he was beginning to move through the crowd, weaving his way towards the staircase, his eyes pinned on hers...

Belle twirled away from the balustrade, fanning anxiously at her suddenly glowing cheeks.

"Belle? Arabella Audley? Oh, is it truly you?"

Someone—not the military gentleman, the voice was too high and piping—called her name from below, in tones equal part eagerness and surprise.

Belle hardly needed the disdainfully raised eyebrow of her mother's uncle, the Duke of Glenlyon, the eldest and most politically influential of her guardians, to remind her it was poor breeding, particularly for a lady, to cry out so, especially in the midst of court.

But while Belle had all due respect for the value of social niceties, it chafed to have to always submit her decidedly strong will to the dictates of the Five Lords of Lectures. Especially as curiosity had always been her besetting sin…

Belle glanced carefully at Glenlyon, then at Lady Mowbray, before finally casting what she hoped appeared to be a careless glance back over the balustrade. And clutched at the handrail when she caught sight of a girl whom she'd not seen since being yanked so unceremoniously from school five years ago—

Patty? Careful to keep her awkwardly wide court hoops from bumping against the other guests waiting on the staircase beside her, Belle rose on her toes to peer over the balustrade. *Patty Jones?*

Patty had been the heart of the Abbey Girls' school, at least during the one short year Belle's guardians had allowed her to attend. A lively, warm-hearted young lady, all wit and spirit, the primary instigator of their many games and schemes. And oh, what stories she could tell!

A grin that felt as bright as a firework flared over Belle's face.

Patty, the mere granddaughter of a baronet, looked not at all daunted to find herself rubbing shoulders with the members of fashionable society, waving up with such vigor Belle feared the yard-long ostrich feathers perched in her golden hair might soon take wing.

Without thinking, Belle's hand rose to wave back, only to halt mid-rise as her eyes caught once again on the scarlet-coated officer.

Who stopped his headlong rush across the vestibule when Patty reached out a hand to stop him. Who now bent his head to listen to her urgently whispered words. Who then placed Patty's gloved hand atop his arm…

"Arabella." Glenlyon's hiss-whisper pressed as heavily on her propriety as his be-ringed hand bore down against her shoulder. "Do not make a spectacle of yourself. You know what is at stake here today."

With appalling inelegance, Belle turned her back once again on the balustrade, her hand jerking back to her side.

How cruel to be forced not to acknowledge an old friend!

And how ridiculous, to feel even a hint of—of whatever was making her hands clench and her teeth grind at the sight of that friend's hand on the arm of the handsome officer…

Andrew Ferguson, Aunt Elizabeth's husband, cleared his throat. "You must remember, my dear Arabella, that today you will make your first impressions on our monarchs, and on those who have their ears. And that first impressions are the most lasting. You would not wish to give the king, or those who influence the king, any cause to judge the future heirs of your body unworthy of the titles, honors, and dignities of your father's earldom."

"Nor the Members of the Lords Committee on Privileges, many of whom will also be in attendance today," the Duke of Glenlyon reminded. "Recall that they, as well as the king, will play a role in deciding whether one of your father's distant male relations should be granted the Audley titles rather than yourself."

Sir Francis Thurlow, her father's maternal cousin, laughed. "The King will sooner grant the American colonies representation in Parliament than allow a female to inherit an English earldom. Far better to ask George to declare the title extinct, and then bestow it upon the man Arabella marries. Especially if that man is an Englishman of influence here at court."

Glenlyon raised a supercilious eyebrow. "You have forgotten,

Thurlow, that the late king promised Arabella's father to ensure a female might once again inherit the Audley title."

In the early sixteenth century, one of Belle's ancestresses *had* inherited the Audley earldom. But soon thereafter, the earldom's letters patent had been amended to ensure such a travesty never occurred again. Unlike the Scottish Culmaily barony, which had passed to her directly upon her father's death, Belle could not currently inherit the Audley earldom. Not unless the king agreed to yet another amendment.

A far from likely occurrence, Belle thought, despite George II's promise to her father. No, a far better way to secure the title would be for her to forge an alliance with one of two distant relations petitioning Parliament for the title.

But none of her guardians, either Scots or English, agreed with Belle. In their minds, it would simply not do to reward a mere commoner presumptuous enough to claim a peerage.

No matter that the claims of both Audley Seagrave and Henry de Audley had some legal merit, at least to Belle's mind.

Sir Francis sniffed. "A loose promise at best. You've nothing in writing."

"Do you discount my influence at court?"

Mowbray waved a dismissive hand. "Just because you and that Northern Machiavel, Lord Bute, are as thick as inkle-weavers—"

"As if our current monarch would care for any promises made by his grandfather! You know George despised him," Sir Francis spoke over Mowbray's, his voice appallingly loud.

Belle curled a hand about the handrail. Had her guardians actually allowed their private squabbling to break out in public? She shot each a cautioning glance, but, as usual, they paid her not the least heed. Too busy with their own petty quarrels to realize they were making far more of a spectacle than Belle ever could…

"Arabella," Aunt Elizabeth said in a carrying voice, clearly attempting to curtail the gentlemen's all-too-familiar feud. "What a becoming color you've chosen for your gown."

Belle restrained a snort. As if her aunt had never before seen it, when she and Lady Mowbray had argued for hours at the mercer's over precisely which fabric to choose!

"Yes, that silvery-blue is a near match to your eyes," Lady Kerr concurred. "And the pattern! Not just the silver balls of a baronage, but the strawberry leaves of an earldom as well? Such fine work must have been commissioned from Lyons."

"Spitalfields silk, just as the queen decrees," Lady Mowbray contradicted, her voice replete with dismissal. "I doubt they've anything as fine in France, not to mention poor backwards Scotland."

And now the ladies were on the verge of making a spectacle of themselves, too…

"Excuse me, please, will you, sir? Oh, thank you, my lady, I'll only be a moment…"

Was that Patty's voice piping over the murmurs of the waiting crowd? Had she miraculously come to Belle's rescue, even after Belle's pained dismissal?

Mimicking Lady Mowbray's affected languor, Belle glanced slowly over her shoulder.

Then pressed the top of her fan against her lips to contain a wayward chuckle. Yes, not only had her friend ignored the cut Belle had been forced to give, she was even now attempting to push her way past the courtiers and aristocrats jealously guarding their places in the queue on the palace's Grand Staircase. How did such a tiny slip of a woman ever hope to accomplish such a feat?

But then a military officer—not the one who had caught Belle's attention, but another, even taller, gentleman—took Patty's arm and began clearing a path for her through the bejeweled, bewigged crowd.

Had she been wrong to assume some intimacy between Patty

and the officer of the broad shoulders?

No. Because there, only a few steps below them, followed the gentleman, apologizing and appeasing the disgruntled courtiers the pair had left in their wake.

"Oh, my dear Belle!" Patty exclaimed as she reached the landing on which their party stood. Then, with no regard for rank or situation, she snatched up Belle's gloved hands and pulled her close, setting a quick kiss against each of her powdered cheeks.

Oh, how good it felt to be greeted as a friend, instead of instructed and criticized and ordered about as if she had no thoughts, no feelings of her own…

"Darling Belle, what a picture you make!" Patty exclaimed as she threw their joined hands out wide, her eyes roving up and down Belle's far taller figure. "And not just because your gown and jewels outshine those of every other lady here. Did I not tell everyone at school that you'd soon grow into your looks?"

Belle's breath, and words, suddenly caught in her throat. Not because of Patty's compliment, outrageous and indiscreet though it might be. Nor because of the obvious disapproval flowing like waves from Glenlyon and the rest of the Squabbling Squadron. And certainly not because of the over-tall man by her friend's side—a husband, perhaps?—whose grin spread almost as wide as Patty's.

No, Belle had been rendered speechless by a pair of ardent green eyes.

The officer's lips—wide, generous lips—quirked in a half-smile as those eyes met Belle's in frank assessment. She felt heat bloom in her cheeks again, but forced her own eyes to narrow. Both Lady Mowbray and Lady Kerr had warned her she must immediately rebuff the attentions of any man presumptuous enough to grin at a gentlewoman to whom he had never been introduced.

"Will you introduce your friends to us, Lady Culmaily?"

Glenlyon asked, clearly making the best of a bad situation. Although the shift of his tone at the word "friends" suggested he was holding judgment on that front for the nonce.

"Yes, of course," she said, striving to gather her composure. "Your grace, Miss Martha Jones, the granddaughter of Sir Thomas Longueville of Wolverton. Patty, my uncle, the Duke of Glenlyon—"

"Oh, it's no longer *Miss*. It's *Mrs.* Astley now," her friend interrupted before making her curtsy to the duke. "May I present my husband, Sergeant Major Philip Astley, late of His Majesty's 15th Light Dragoons?"

Glenlyon gave the slightest bow in return, the corner of his eyebrow giving a small but significant hitch at the sound of the name. Was Patty's husband a soldier of some renown?

"And that rascal behind him is his most particular friend, Captain Rye," Patty added.

Captain *Rye*. Belle pressed her closed fan against her ribs. Of course the handsome stranger wasn't Henry de Audley. How silly to think for even a moment he could possibly be one of the men upon whom she must set her matrimonial sights.

The captain, seemingly more familiar with court etiquette than Patty, offered their group a smart bow. "Your Grace," he said, his voice an unexpectedly smoky rumble. A rumble that resonated deep inside Belle, as if someone had set a pianoforte inside her and struck a chord on its lowest-noted keys.

Belle cleared her throat. "Mrs. Astley, Sergeant Major Astley, Captain Rye, may I present Lord and Lady Mowbray, Sir Francis Thurlow, Sir Alexander and Lady Kerr, and Mr. Andrew and Lady Elizabeth Ferguson?"

Why were Lady Mowbray and Lady Kerr frowning so? Oh, merciful heavens! Had she introduced the higher-ranking ladies to Patty and her party, instead of the other way round?

"Lady Elizabeth is my father's sister," Belle added, hoping to distract them from her painful faux pas.

"Oh, Aunt Elizabeth! How pleased I am to meet you!" Patty enthused. "Belle told me so much about you when we were at school together, I feel as if you are my favorite aunt, too."

Captain Rye's lips quirked, a breathtakingly disarming half-smile. Not as if he were laughing at Belle's social slip, but inviting her to share his amusement at Patty's inadvertent indiscretions. Tempting Belle to share some private pleasure all their own…

Belle managed to squelch the urge to smile back at him in return. But she could not seem to control her hand, which waved her fan once again with unbecoming vigor. How else was she to keep the color suddenly flooding her cheeks in check?

A commotion at the top of the staircase distracted the party before any of her guardians could chastise her for allowing a complete stranger to throw her into such obvious confusion.

Thank heavens! The crowd ahead of them had finally begun to move.

"If you would excuse us?" Glenlyon nodded to Patty and the officers, then held out his arm to Belle. "Lady Culmaily, it is time."

Time, yes. Time to set her audacious plan in motion. A plan from which she would not allow a far-too-charming stranger to divert her.

Belle gave a graceful nod to her old friend, then squared her shoulders, raised her chin, and set her fingertips atop Glenlyon's silk sleeve.

Time to take control of her own life. Time to show the English court that Arabella Audley was worthy not only of the barony of Culmaily, but of the dignities, honours, and privileges of her father's Audley earldom, too.

Even if she had to marry to gain them.

Belle drew in a deep, determined breath as a yeoman usher opened the door at the top of the Grand Staircase. That door would not provide immediate access to the Royal presence, as Belle's guardians had continually reminded her. No, she and her party, just like the rest of the buzzing crowd, must first pass through an enfilade of apartments, beginning with the King's Guard Room.

At first glance, an austere chamber, with few furnishings beyond a table and several chairs set in front of the large Portland stone chimneypiece with a black marble shelf. But above the wainscoting, swords and muskets and pistols arranged in ornamental swirls, braids, and crosses created both an aesthetic and a symbolic display, signaling to all visitors the power and might of the British monarchy. As did the dozens of Yeomen of the Guard lining the chamber, pikes raised at attention.

A martial display meant to awe, even to intimidate. But it took more than mere show to make Arabella Audley quaver.

Or to cow Captain Rye. Behind her, she heard him greet several of the guards with friendly affability, even with warmth. Was he a frequent visitor to court?

"Come along, Arabella," Lady Mowbray said, taking Belle's arm in a controlling grip. "We've several more chambers to traverse before we reach the royal presence, and we wouldn't wish you to swoon from the heat or the press of the crowd before you've even had a chance to be introduced to the queen."

Belle gave a curt nod. Purposeless, such curiosity about a stranger. She'd not come to court to moon over a handsome face…

Yet something in her body remained poised, too aware, of the party behind them as Lady Mowbray hurried Belle towards the gentleman usher guarding the entrance to yet another room.

Their attire and bearing must have passed muster (and the vail Glenlyon offered must have been large enough) for the usher to admit their group without question to the next room, the Presence Chamber. The weapons of the Guard Room had been replaced here by heavy tapestries and ancestral portraits, a display of a different kind of authority and power. A power her father had taken similar pains to evoke in the public rooms at both Audley Priory and Culmaily Castle.

Glenlyon nudged her elbow, a reminder of the necessity of curtsying three times as they passed the throne that stood at the end of the room, even though no one occupied it. Yet another way for the monarch to impress upon visitors his supremacy and will.

A groom turned aside several unworthies before allowing Belle's party to pass into the Privy Chamber; a similar ritual, performed this time by a gentleman usher, was repeated at the entrance to the King's Withdrawing Room.

Here, the grand, the near-grand, and the wishing-to-be-granted-grandiosity thronged, the sound of greetings both hearty and insincere near deafening. Beside her, Lady Mowbray and Aunt Elizabeth whispered the names and ranks of the courtiers crowding about them, pointing out who was worth knowing, and who was not. Glenlyon went in search of the Lord Chamberlain to request an introduction for her to the king and queen.

While they waited for the monarchs, Belle glanced about the small room with eager curiosity. Were either of the men she sought in attendance? Challenging, it was, to maneuver about the cramped space without bumping into the other ladies' wide hoops or treading on their trains. Even more challenging to see through the waving, semi-diaphanous screen of dipping and bobbing ostrich plumes, which every lady was required to wear atop her head. And the air here felt even more stifling than it had on the staircase—

Belle stilled as Lord Mowbray placed a hand on her shoulder and gave her a warning squeeze.

"Seagrave," he said with icy politeness to someone standing behind her. "We did not expect to see you at court today."

Belle's heart pounded. She counted slowly to five before turning to face Audley Seagrave, one of the two men whom she must take to husband.

"Mowbray. Thurlow." The tall, almost emaciated elderly man bowed with stiff formality. As he rose, Belle searched his features for some similarity to her father's, or to the ancestral portraits in the gallery at Audley Priory. But the gentleman must have taken after his mother's side of the family, for of her father's genial blue eyes, Romanesque nose, and perpetually upturned lips she could find no sign.

Belle's heart sunk. Audley Seagrave looked far older than his nearly sixty years. Would he even be able to father a child?

"Is not the king's birthday temptation enough to visit London?" the older man asked, a not-entirely kind smile snaking over his face. "Even if the Committee on Privileges had not finally scheduled a time for petitioners to the Audley earldom to present their cases in rebuttal of yours."

"The Committee has set a date for the next hearing?" Belle exclaimed, shooting a glance between Lord Mowbray and Sir Francis.

The former's expression remained unmoved, but the way Sir Francis's eyes skittered away from hers betrayed the truth.

They had known, but not seen fit to inform her. As if it were not the least concern of hers.

As if she were a mere pawn in the game…

"This is the chit, I take it?" Seagrave's eyes shifted from bland politeness to curious speculation as they turned to Belle.

Lord Mowbray nodded. "Lady Culmaily, may I present your father's cousin, Mr. Audley Seagrave?"

Belle forced a civil smile and held out a hand.

"Lady Culmaily." The older man pressed his lips to her glove, then raised his eyes to hers. A surprisingly disarming twinkle lit those hazel eyes as he added, "And perhaps, one day, Lady Audley, too, if you choose to form a propitious alliance?"

"Perhaps," Belle answered, her pulse quickening. The scheduled Parliamentary hearing might prove entirely unnecessary, if the gentleman were thinking along the same lines as she…

"An alliance with an Englishman of influence here at court would be very welcome," Lord Mowbray interposed, his posture as stiff as his tone.

"Or the king might recommend that the letters patent be amended to allow a female to inherit in her own right," Uncle Andrew added, his voice equally cold.

But the older man only shook his head. "I did advise your father not to drop the noble name of Seagrave, my dear, and resume one unassociated with our family since the days of the Tudors. A change of name does not make it any more likely our monarch will grant the Audley title to a female, even one as prettyish as yourself."

"Our new king has granted peerages to several ladies during his short tenure, I understand," Belle declared.

"To the wives and widows of political leaders, perhaps," he conceded with a nod. "But with honors only to be succeeded by males of their lines."

How gratifying to find Seagrave directing his comments not to her guardians, but to her.

"What of Lady Townshend?" Aunt Elizabeth's gentle voice inquired. "I do not believe her husband held a position in government."

"Yes, did the king not grant her the Greenwich title?" Belle challenged, surprised to find herself enjoying verbally sparring with the gentleman. Perhaps being married to an older man would not prove so very difficult.

Seagrave humphed. "A mere barony, not her father's dukedom. And the Greenwich titles had no extant males of the line to inherit. Unlike the Audley earldom."

Glenlyon rejoined their party, shooting a glance of clear disdain at the interloper. "It is too bad, is it not, Seagrave, that the English look so askance at those of us with Scots blood? Especially those whose relations supported the Jacobite cause. If only your grandfather's baronetcy had not been attainted, your claim to the Audley title might already have been granted."

Belle's hands clenched. Oh, why must her guardians take such a haughty, dismissive tone with the man?

"Might you be considering a propitious alliance of your own, Sir Audley?" Belle asked, granting the gentleman the courtesy of the title that should have been his. "With a prettyish sort of young lady?"

The elderly man barked out a laugh. "Me, my dear? Why, I'm far too old to want some bothersome female lording it over my breakfast table every morning, or making demands of me in bed every night."

Belle let her hand slip from the man's arm. Had she mistaken his intent?

"However," he said with a surprisingly engaging grin, "I could not say the same for my grandson—"

He broke off at a sudden stirring by the door, which drew the attention of the entire room. The king's and queen's attendants, followed by the monarchs themselves, had finally arrived.

"Excuse me, my dear. Shall we resume our conversation at another, more propitious time?" Seagrave whispered in Belle's ear. "At tonight's birthday ball, perhaps? My grandsons and I have been invited to attend. As have you, I assume?"

"Indeed, sir. I would welcome it," Belle whispered back.

Seagrave stepped away as Belle's party, along with the rest of the crowd, hurriedly arranged themselves in a semicircle, waiting for a turn to greet the monarchs.

The gentleman had grandsons? She'd never considered the possibility of forging an alliance not with Seagrave himself, but with one of his male progeny....

Not as direct a path to her father's title, wedding the eldest grandson rather than the man himself. Even so, Belle was pleased to have another option to consider. If Audley Seagrave refused to marry, and Henry de Audley, the other claimant petitioning Parliament for the Audley earldom, proved unsuitable, it might be her only chance to gain the title.

Across the room, she watched Patty fussing at her husband, reaching up a gloved hand to untangle the fringe of one of his dress uniform's epaulettes. Captain Rye, standing to Astley's other side, mimicked Patty to comic effect.

If only this grandson proved half as compelling as the playful captain...

A gentle nudge against her arm from Aunt Elizabeth shook Belle from her reverie. Yes, now was not the time to allow her mind to wander, not when she would soon make her bow to the monarchs.

Belle watched with interest as Queen Charlotte curtsied to her king, then turned to greet the party at the left side of the semicircle, the silver tissue of the train of her formal gown gathered up and held by a Lady of the Bedchamber. King George, resplendent in purple for the celebration of his birthday, moved to the right.

Belle slipped a hand inside her pocket, smoothing a finger against her mother's brooch. The late Lady Audley had pinned it to John's, and then to Belle's, baby skirts, a talisman meant to ward against the evil eye.

"Do not alarm yourself, my dear," Lady Mowbray whispered.

"Our queen is noted for her good humor and lively but equable temper."

"If not for her ravishing beauty," Lady Kerr murmured.

No, not a beauty, their German queen. But despite her unfortunately large, upturned nose and rather pointed chin, the welcoming smile she offered each visitor she greeted suggested a pleasant, agreeable temper. Only a few years older than Belle, their queen had already given birth to five children, four of them boys. Male heirs enough to ensure the continuance of her husband's line—

"Remember not to turn your back to her, or to the king," Uncle Andrew whispered as the Queen and her Lord Chamberlain, moving far more slowly than the King, began to traverse the semicircle.

"And do not forget to remove your right-hand glove before she reaches us," Lady Mowbray added. "But do not kiss her hand; only ladies under the rank of right honorable are required to do so."

"Offer her your deepest curtsey," Glenlyon said.

"Remember to allow her to speak first, and ask no questions," Lord Kerr cautioned.

"But when she speaks to you, be sure not to answer with mere monosyllables," Lady Mowbray warned. "Impress her with your wit, as there is nothing she finds so hard to discover at court as good conversation."

Belle sighed and nodded. Would her Clucking Caretakers never stop offering advice? She'd studied proper court protocol for months!

Her attention fixed on the king, who, with a gentleman of the royal bedchamber beside him—the Duke of Richmond, Belle thought—exchanged a few pleasantries with Audley Seagrave, then passed quickly on to the next party, and the next. But then he stopped altogether, clapping his hands in delight. What personage could capture the monarch's attention so decidedly?

Belle craned her neck to see over the lilting plumes. Happily, a gentleman in front of her bent to speak with his companion, offering Belle a clear view of the group who had caught the king's attention. Patty's companions!

"Sergeant Major Philip Astley, formerly of Your Majesty's Regiment of Light Dragoons, and his wife, Mrs. Martha Astley," Richmond read off a card Astley had handed him. "And Captain —"

"Astley? Was it not Astley who presented us with the captured colors from the battle of Emsdorf?" the king interrupted, his ruddy complexion growing even redder under the white curls of his short wig.

"Indeed, Your Majesty," Astley said after he, Patty, and Captain Rye offered obeisance to the sovereign. "It was the greatest honor of my life to lay those colors at your feet."

"And you, Captain," the king continued, turning his blue-grey gaze on the other officer. "Reports inform us of your bravery during that same engagement. Charged the enemy lines single-handedly, did you not?"

Captain Rye inclined his head. "Your Majesty is too kind. Any other English soldier would have done the same."

"Well said, Captain, well said!" the king enthused. "It is loyal, dutiful men such yourself who make our army the envy of the world."

Belle's stomach gave an unexpected flutter. Not just any officer, Patty's Captain Rye, but one whose heroism had been marked enough to come to the attention of the king!

King George stood taller than most of the gentlemen in the room, but both Patty's husband and Captain Rye surpassed him.

"Richmond, did we hear you say 'formerly'?" The king's high forehead wrinkled. "Are you no longer in our service, Astley?"

"As a married gentleman yourself, Your Majesty, surely you must understand my wish to spend as much time as possible with my new bride," Patty's husband offered with a charming waggle of his eyebrows.

"Especially a bride as lovely as yours," the king acknowledged with an appreciative glance at Patty. "And what of you, Captain? Have you followed our example and taken a lady of good standing to wife?"

The captain's gaze darted to the right, where the queen stood conversing with a party of Frenchmen. "Alas, my king, I have not yet been blessed to find a *parti* as lively and good-tempered as yours."

But rather than resting on the queen, the captain's eyes continued to search the room.

And halted when they met Belle's…

An unfamiliar mixture of embarrassment and confusion sent her own eyes lowering to the floor. But she could not help but hear the amusement in the king's voice as he offered his well-wishes for the Captain's search.

"She'll have to be a lady who loves horses, will she not, Rye?" Patty exclaimed.

Belle's eyes jerked up at this unexpected feminine interjection in the gentlemen's conversation.

"For my husband has recently opened a riding school, Your Majesty," Patty brashly continued. "And he's been developing a new form of entertainment, too—performances of horsemanship and acrobatics that we believe will delight audiences all across London, if not the entire country. Captain Rye has been kind enough to lend us his assistance for the nonce."

Riding school? *Performances?* Belle's eyes shot between Astley, Patty, and Captain Rye. What—*who?*—had her friend married?

The king's auburn eyebrows rose. "Indeed? Perhaps one day we shall invite him to perform—"

"Your Majesty?" Richmond interrupted, darting an anxious glance around the half-circle of as-yet-to-be-greeted guests, and then towards Queen Charlotte. "We would not wish the queen to grow weary."

"Ah, bless me, no. Breeding again, poor dear. Best move along, eh? Good-day to you, Sergeant, Captain. Mrs. Astley—"

A yank on Belle's elbow jerked her attention back to her own party. All of whose members, she saw with dismay, were bowing and curtsying to the queen…

Belle lowered into her most graceful obeisance, grateful that Glenlyon had moved to partially shield her from the monarch's view.

"We are knowing most of your party, Your Grace," the queen said, tilting her powdered, pearled-adorned head towards Glenlyon. "But who is the lovely young dame?"

Belle's mouth grew dry as the queen's Chamberlain, Earl Harcourt, glanced down at a card in his hand. "The Right Honorable the Baroness Culmaily, presented by her aunt, the Lady Elizabeth Ferguson."

Remembering proper protocol, Belle drew off her right glove and lowered even further to the floor.

"*Baroness*? *Freifrau* Culmaily? Or *Freiin*?" the queen asked, the short, sharp vowels and the unfamiliar words an obvious reminder of her foreign birth.

"Not the wife of a baron, Your Majesty," Belle said as she rose, taking advantage of the studies in German her father had insisted she undertake. "I am as yet unmarried. Nor daughter, either, or not only so. You see, I hold my late father's barony in my own right."

The queen turned to her Chamberlain, brow wrinkling. "In her own right? A female? But how could that be so?"

The Chamberlain looked pained. "Some Scots titles may be inherited through the female line, Your Majesty. Lady Culmaily's late father held both the barony of Culmaily and the earldom of Audley."

"Earldom?" The queen frowned. "Is she not *Gräfin*, then?"

"No, Your Majesty," the Chamberlain said with a sniff.

"English titles rarely pass through the female line."

"The succession of my father's earldom is currently in dispute," Belle added.

The queen laid a hand on Belle's arm, her expression filled with pity. "What a terrible tangle for an unwed girl. A lady needs a husband to deal with such troublesome matters for her. *Mein Schatz*, we advise you to marry, and at once."

"That is my wish as well, Your Majesty," Belle said, even though her reasons for wanting a spouse differed from the queen's.

"Then you must—"

A gasp from the other side of the drawing room brought the queen's words to an abrupt halt. Alarm rippled the room at the sight of the king, a hand pressed to his nose, blood oozing from between his fingers.

"His Majesty is unwell," she heard the Duke of Richmond exclaim. "He must retire at once."

"*On our Lord Jesus' grave spring three roses—the first is Hope, the second Patience, the third God's Will: blood, I pray you be still!*" the queen murmured. "A handkerchief, Harcourt. *Sofort!*"

Belle blinked, hardly able to believe her eyes as the monarchs and their attendants rushed from the room. "What happened?"

"A mere bleeding of the nose," Glenlyon said, his words short and clipped. "Prone to them, the king is, I understand. Embarrassing for a ruler to show even that little weakness, especially in the midst of court, but hardly debilitating. Come, there will be no more chance this afternoon to make our case."

And just like that, the Birthday Drawing Room was over.

Belle tried not to allow disappointment to overtake her as Glenlyon set her hand on his arm and retraced their steps through the suite of royal apartments. "Will this evening's Birthday Ball be deferred, do you think?"

"Over such a silly trifle?" Glenlyon snorted. "Now that

would truly be an embarrassment."

Belle allowed a sigh to escape. At least she'd have another opportunity to broach her scheme to the king.

"Arabella!" Lady Mowbray exclaimed, pausing at the top of the Grand Staircase. "Why have you only one glove?"

Belle stopped and raised her hands, the left encased in white kid, the other embarrassingly bare. Where could her other glove have gone?

"You removed it when you made your obeisance to the queen," Aunt Elizabeth reminded in a whisper. "You should have put it back on when we left the Drawing Room."

Belle thrust a hand into one hoop pocket, and then the other, but of the errant glove there was no sign. "I must have dropped it."

Lord Mowbray gave an imperious wave. "Send one of the guards to retrieve it."

"But I know just where I was standing. It will be faster if I go myself."

"My dear Lady Culmaily! I hardly think—"

But the rest of Lady Kerr's protest vanished in the din as Belle rushed off, swimming against the tide of the departing crowd. Back through the Guard Room, the Presence Chamber and Privy Chamber, until she caught sight of the faded crimson curtains, the tarnished silver-gilt chandelier, and the staid portraits of the King's Withdrawing Room. Yes, there, right where she had curtsied to the queen, Belle spied a spill of white kid on the gleaming wooden floor.

Trying to appear as unobtrusive as possible, Belle inched past the handful of courtiers who had still not left the apartment, then knelt down to where her glove had lain. A difficult feat, with such wide skirts and hoops, but somehow she managed to touch the floor.

But instead of cool kid, her fingers met warm, living flesh.

A hand far larger than hers, palms and finger pads rough

with calluses, grasped hers and drew her upright.

She stared at the high, tanned forehead, the tousled brown curls glinting in the sunlight flooding in from the south-facing windows, the green eyes animated with the keenest of interest as they roved across her face.

"Captain Rye." Good heavens, surely her voice had not wavered…

"Lady Culmaily," he said, his own voice tauntingly calm. "A vital element of your court caparison seems to have gone astray."

"Yours as well, captain," she replied, casting a significant glance down at their bare—and still-entwined—hands.

But neither her raised eyebrow nor her subtle rebuke seemed to disconcert him at all. At least not enough to remember his manners and release her hand.

She could always pull hers from his. But was that not just what he wished, for his own provoking behavior to provoke her?

Besides, she had no wish to show the presumptuous fellow how much the mere touch of his hand was affecting her.

What was it about this soldier, that such a touch could make not just her fingers, but her entire person prick with unfamiliar awareness?

"Ah, but I know where *my* glove has gone—right into my left-hand pocket, alongside its mate. Too warm today to keep the hands covered a moment longer than necessary, do you not agree? I wonder, though—are you aware of the fate of yours?"

The smile on those generous lips, the gleam of amusement in those green eyes—why, the man was not simply trying to provoke her. He was actually *flirting* with her!

Lady Kerr and Lady Mowbray, for once putting aside their differences, had both warned Belle against the coquetries in which men at court were all too wont to indulge. But she'd paid them scant mind, certain that the proper dignity of her own behavior would discourage any such advances, or make them easy to instantly check.

Yet here she was, still allowing a man she barely knew to hold her ungloved hand in his…

"I suspect, sir, a scoundrel has absconded with it," she replied. "But he may prove himself worthy of a more respectable sobriquet by returning said object to its rightful owner."

"Or perhaps he glories in the epithet. Perhaps he means to retain the glove as a sign of the lady's favor."

"Favor? When the item was stolen away without her knowledge? Hardly a sign of freely bestowed regard."

"But perhaps the scoundrel does not wish the lady to know of his devotion. Perhaps he fears his feelings are unrequited."

"Or perhaps he fears the wrath of her five guardians, should they discover the rogue importuning her in such an impertinent manner?"

"Five? *Five* guardians?" Captain Rye's eyebrows rose to an almost absurd degree.

Belle could hardly believe Patty had failed to inform him of the fact. Still, she felt her lips quirk at his exaggerated show of dismay. "Not just five guardians, but three of their wives, as well," she added with a wry smile.

The gold buttons on the captain's uniform jiggled as he gave a comically exaggerated shudder. "And here I thought being subject to the constant demands of a grandfather and an elder brother an intolerable burden. No wonder you've slipped the reins…."

Belle's smile disappeared. "I might not feel the need to 'slip the reins' if I still had a father or elder brother to act on my behalf."

He blinked and dropped her hand, obviously surprised by the sudden shift from dalliance to dismay.

She took a step back and bit her lip.

From the pocket of his gleaming white waistcoat, he pulled her missing glove and pressed it into her palm. "Forgive me, my lady. I may have lost my parents many years ago, but I well remember the sting of grief."

"Rye?" Belle heard Patty's voice pipe from behind her. "My apologies for sending you on a fool's errand. I found it right here, in my pocket."

Belle glanced over her shoulder to find her old friend waving a glove of her own in the air, a triumphant gleam in her eye.

"And Belle, what luck!" Patty grasped Belle's hand, lacing together their fingers. "Did you see what happened? Poor King George, I do hope he will be all right. But I can't help but be glad that the Drawing Room broke up early, for that means you will have time to attend our performance this afternoon!"

"My dear Patty, you can hardly expect Lady Culmaily to attend an exhibition on such short notice," Captain Rye protested.

"Oh, pish! What might be short notice to others is nothing to a loyal friend. Belle, will you not come?" Patty exclaimed, laying her free hand on Belle's sleeve. "As a special favor to me?"

"I wish I could, Patty. But I don't know…"

"We're not far away, just at Halfpenny Hatch," Patty encouraged, just as she had whenever Belle had wavered in the face of one of her friend's audacious schemes back at school.

Belle sighed. Oh, how lovely to escape the weight and worries of the day, even for a few hours. And how dashing Captain Rye would look, performing feats of daring atop a handsome steed.

Perhaps Patty would even give Belle a chance to try one of their horses herself…

"Attend an exhibition? Today, when we've the birthday ball for which to prepare?"

The disapproval in Lord Mowbray's voice jerked Belle out of her daydream. She looked over her shoulder again and saw her eight Meddlesome Mentors, *all* of whom appeared to have come after her.

"Halfpenny Hatch? Why, that's clear across the river!" Lord Kerr exclaimed.

"I hardly think such a performance suitable for a gentlewoman," Lady Mowbray added.

"No Scottish lady of my acquaintance would dare attend such a display," Lady Kerr nodded, for once in agreement with her English counterpart.

"Perhaps we might call on you at home some other day, Mrs. Astley," Aunt Elizabeth said, her tone apologetic.

Belle's fingers clenched about the glove in her hand. The constant carping of her guardians—the rising anxiety, then unexpected deflation, of her first court visit—the quick flash of hurt on Patty's face—the hint of disdain on Captain Rye's, which had displaced the eager interest which had earlier animated his mobile features—too much, all too much for propriety to keep properly in check.

"Thank you, Patty, for your kind invitation," Belle said as she took her old friend's hand in hers. "I would be overjoyed to attend your performance."

ASTLEY'S RIDING SCHOOL

Southwark, Halfpenny Hatch
Late afternoon

Belle's gloved hand gripped the edge of the window of Glenlyon's carriage as it trundled over the recently built Westminster Bridge, then turned sharply north. Free for a few hours from the full force of her Eight Pillars of Propriety, since Lady Mowbray and Lord and Lady Kerr had all chosen not to attend Astley's performance.

How different, this part of the city, as compared to Mayfair and St. James's! Physical labor, rather than the political and social posturing of the *ton*, appeared to be the order of the day in Southwark. Men sifted and shoveled coal from barges lining the wharves, or stacked timber shipped from the colonies into neat piles, ready to be collected by the builders and architects who would transform it into houses, sailing ships, and even decorative furniture. Women bustled between the attached houses snaking about the curving road opposite, hanging out laundry, carrying the marketing, chasing and chastising the young children who played about their feet.

So different in dress and speech from those who worked the lands about Audley Priory, tilling and seeding its soil every spring, gathering the fruits of its growing every autumn! But perhaps not so different, either, men and women all relying on the integrity and good business sense of those who owned the places where they toiled, as Audley Priory's laborers had once depended on her father, and, after her father's death, on Lord

Mowbray and his steward, whom her guardians had agreed would direct the estate on her behalf. And, in future, on whomever would be named Earl of Audley in her father's place.

As the carriage took another turn, this time towards the east, the stink of smoke and sawdust abruptly gave way to a far more familiar scent: the earthy vegetation of market gardens and fields, the sweet fragrance of orchards of apple, pear, and plum. Of course, the people of London, just like those of Leicestershire, all needed to eat...

On the seat beside her, Sir Francis gave a delicate, almost pained, sniff as a stronger, far more pungent scent than that of growing things suddenly wafted through the lowered window.

"Belvedere's Brewery to your right. And Beaufoy's Vinegar Manufactory to the left." Glenlyon waved a careless hand. "Southwark supplies more than just produce for the denizens of London."

Belle gave her eldest guardian a grateful smile. Not just for the explanation, but for his surprising support of her desire to attend Astley's exhibition. After her impetuous acceptance of Patty's invitation, she'd expected her guardians to hurry her away, and then to inform her in no uncertain terms that she must send Mrs. Astley her regrets. The polite but insincere apology she would have to write had already been forming in her head when Glenlyon stepped forward to second her acceptance and make inquiries about the time and location of Astley's performance.

"It seems an odd place to set up a riding exhibition," Belle said as the carriage slowed. "Will the *ton* come all the way over the river to see such a thing?"

"The south bank has long played host to entertainments unable, or unwilling, to beg a license from the Lord Chamberlain," Glenlyon said.

"Yes, when we were at Oxford, your father and I dashed up when we heard two monstrous dromedaries, a she-camel and her young one, had just arrived from Tartary." Lord Mowbray's usually stern mouth quirked in happy remembrance. "Seven foot high, and ten foot long, the dam was, if she was an inch!"

Lord Mowbray and Sir Francis began to reminisce about their youthful exploits among the entertainments of the south bank. Belle turned back to the open window, then smiled as she caught sight of Patty's husband, looking quite imposing atop a tall white charger, cavalry sword in hand. With that sword, he directed their carriage to follow several others past another orchard, toward a rough-hewn set of stables.

After their driver brought the horses to a halt, Glenlyon handed her down from the carriage. Belle's boots sank into the grassy sward next to a small piece of ground which had been enclosed behind a paling of thin, waist-high branches whittled free of their bark. On the side of the stables, a hand-painted banner proclaimed "Astley's Riding School" in bold block letters.

Most of the attendees of the performance appeared to be gentlemen, but Belle and Aunt Elizabeth were not the only ladies of quality in the crowd. She even spied one or two whom she recognized from the Royal Drawing Room earlier in the day. Ha! What would Lady Mowbray and Lady Kerr say to that?

"Sir Francis!" A spindly young man waved a small bouquet of flowers in the direction of their party. At Sir Francis's nod of acknowledgement, the fellow detached himself from a group of other young gentlemen and minced across the paddock toward their party.

"I did not expect to see you here today, not with the King's birthday ball this evening," the gentleman said as he dipped his head toward Sir Francis. "If *I* had an invitation, as I hear you have been fortunate enough to receive, I would have spent the entire day, nay, the entire week, in preparation!"

Belle could well believe it. She had changed into a riding habit and boots for Astley's performance, but this fellow was rigged out as if he were attending a court ball. His tight-fitting silk jacket of peacock green and waistcoat of the brightest of yellow nearly blinded. He wore not his own hair, but a wig so towering she feared it might catch on a branch of the apple tree growing by the side of the stables. And his scent! Whether it came from the enormous nosegay he held in his hand, the handkerchief half-hanging out of his pocket, or his person itself, a nose-wrinkling combination of every essence in Mr. Warren's perfume shop made her nostrils flare. All paste, powder, and perfume, this fellow was. She'd never seen—nor sniffed—such a display in all the course of her life.

"Sir Henry." Francis Thurlow acknowledged with a wry smile. "Back from the Continent already, are you?"

"Indeed, sir. A sore trial to leave the delights of Italian cuisine, especially when faced with the appalling excuse for cookery one is forced to *manger* here in London. But my solicitor begged my presence, as he believes the House of Peers will hold a hearing about my petition any day now."

Sir Henry? A petition to the House of Peers? Could this be Henry de Audley, the second man who claimed a right to her father's title? If so, his presence confirmed Audley Seagrave's assertion that Parliament was soon to take up the issue of her father's rightful heir.

How like the Lords, to endlessly drag their feet over the case, then rush to render a decision just when Belle needed more time to woo and win a husband…

"And how will you enjoy country life, sir, if your petition is granted?" Sir Francis asked, casting a suspiciously amused glance at Belle. "What pleasure to take to the fields alongside Audley Priory's farmers! And instruct them on the most up-to-date methods of breeding cattle and sheep that you must have learned during your extensive travels! Oh, how I envy you, sir."

The fellow's eyes had grown wider and wider with each of Sir Francis's exclamations. "As if I would ever expose a countenance I have taken such pains to keep pale to the depredations of the sun! Or soil these soft hands with the stink of livestock. No, I will employ a steward to look to such things, as any man of gentility would."

Or, perhaps, a wife?

"You will reside primarily in town, then?" Uncle Andrew asked.

"Or on the Continent. Even the myriad wonders of London pale after a few months' residence."

A husband who flitted from country to country on the continent, leaving her behind in England? Hardly an ideal marriage, that. Certainly not anything like the loving union of two devoted, even occasionally besotted, consorts she'd witnessed firsthand in the relationship of her mother and father.

Still, one she could learn to tolerate, if it would allow her to take charge of all the day-to-day decisions about Audley Priory herself. Perhaps it wouldn't be necessary to wed Audley Seagrave's grandson and wait to gain her father's title. Not if she could bring this macaroni-man to the point...

"You will risk being cheated, employing a steward and overseeing him from a distance?" Sir Francis asked, then answered his own question before the other man had a chance to answer. "Ah, but if you were to marry—then, sir, you could leave the running of your estate to your wife."

"My wife?" The man's theatrical shudder would have done Garrick proud. "You've never burdened yourself with such an appalling expense, Thurlow. Why would you be so unkind as to wish such a nightmare on me?"

Belle frowned. Surely the fellow could not be in earnest? What gentleman did not wish to marry?

"But one cannot have children—at least, not legitimate ones —without a wedding," Sir Francis said, his butter-wouldn't-melt-in-his-mouth expression comically at odds with the spark of humor in his eyes. "To whom will you leave the title and the estate if you have neither wife nor offspring?"

"What care I for the future?" Sir Henry sniffed. "*Carpe diem quad minimum credula postero*, as the poet reminds us. No, if my petition proves successful, I will drink deeply of as many pleasures as I can, with no thought to hoarding and holding for a tomorrow when I will be dead in the ground."

Belle took a step back. A man who did not wish to marry, who cared more for appeasing his own hedonistic desires than for his good name or the reputation of his family—no, she could never be content to cede the care of the lives and livelihoods of the tenants and workers of the Audley estate to such a selfish creature.

Her abrupt movement must have caught the self-centered man's eye. "But blast me," he exclaimed, turning to her with an elaborate bow. "We need not talk of such things here, especially in the presence of such an exquisitely dressed specimen. Why, I might almost believe myself at the French court again, in the presence of such a surpassing vision of loveliness. Although I would recommend a more striking jewel than the small trinket she currently wears. Why, one can barely see it amid the folds of her fichu!"

Belle's hand flew to her mother's brooch. What an impertinent, vain fellow he was!

"As well as a stronger hand with the rouge; no lady in Paris would take a step outside her boudoir with such unpainted cheeks. I beg you would do me the honor of introducing us, sir."

A wicked twinkle lit Sir Francis's eye. "Certainly, sir. Arabella, may I present Sir Henry de Audley? Sir Henry, Arabella Audley, Baroness Cumaily, and daughter of the late Earl of Audley."

Color even more red than the patches of rouge on Sir Henry's cheekbones flamed across the fellow's entire face. "Oh, my dear lady. What an appalling *faux pas*! I did not think you would be in town—"

"Is not the king's birthday temptation enough to visit

London?" Belle asked. "Even if the Committee on Privileges had not finally scheduled a time for petitioners for my father's earldom to present their cases?"

Sir Francis chuckled at her deliberate echo of Audley Seagrave's words.

But Sir Henry only looked confused. "The King's ball? *You've* received an invitation, as well as Sir Francis?"

"Indeed. A pity you yourself will not have the opportunity to speak with our monarchs about your petition, is it not? Unlike Sir Francis and the rest of my guardians."

"Sir Francis—he is one of your guardians?" Sir Henry bobbed and blinked, giving him the appearance of an alarmingly underfed pigeon. "Why did my solicitor not inform me?"

Beside her, her father's cousin tried, with little success, to suppress a snort.

Glenlyon, who had gone in search of seats for the performance, returned just in time to gift the embarrassed gentleman the most contemptuous of looks. "De Audley. If you will excuse us, sir, I believe the performance is soon to begin. This way, my lady."

Belle took Glenlyon's arm, struggling to keep from catching what would certainly be Sir Francis's satirical eye.

"What a contemptible creature an Englishman dwindles into, when he adopts the follies and vices of other nations," Glenlyon sniffed as he led Belle and the rest of the party away from de Audley.

"What is the world coming to, that a fribble such as *that* would presume to claim an earldom?" Mowbray exclaimed.

"The trifling and eccentric are just as entitled to inherit as the earnest, as long as the blood runs true," Sir Francis objected.

Bell could not help but chuckle as Sir Francis's opinion set off the Squabbling Sentinels again. Eccentric indeed! At least this time, they were not squabbling over her...

Glenlyon led her over a dry dirt track toward a small

pavilion that looked like it had been only recently built. A large circle, set off by stakes and a rope, stood before it. "We may watch the performance free from the glare of the sun here," he said, passing some coins to a boy at the pavilion's entrance, then ushering her towards a raw plank bench still redolent of pitch.

"A ring? Is he to ride in a circle, then, not a straight line?" Uncle Andrew asked.

"How very unusual!" Sir Francis exclaimed, raising an eyeglass to examine the hard-packed track as Belle and her aunt sat on the bench and settled their skirts out of the way.

"Look! There! A rider!" a voice in the crowd exclaimed, sending a shiver of expectation through the gathering. As one, the crowd turned toward the far end of the circular ride. But when it became clear that the horseman was only a young stableboy, expectation quickly abated.

At least for most of the audience. Not, though, for Belle. She laced her gloved hands tight in her lap, forcing herself to sit as still as possible despite the anticipatory tingle racing over her entire person at the prospect of seeing not Patty's husband, but Captain Rye. Ridiculous to feel so, when she'd last seen the gentleman only a few hours earlier…

"Far more people in attendance here than at St. James's this morning," Uncle Andrew said.

"Several hundred, I'd wager," Lord Mowbray agreed.

"If each pays a shilling for the privilege, and extra for a seat in the pavilion, why, Astley could earn a dozen guineas or more every day!" Uncle Andrew calculated. "Quite a lucrative endeavor for a non-commissioned officer."

Belle's head turned at the sound of stable doors opening and the beat of hooves trotting against the hard-packed dirt. Voices around her echoed her barely restrained excitement as a single horseman emerged, guiding his spirited white horse with skill to the circular ride.

Belle's insides fluttered when Patty's husband and his high-spirited steed reached the center of the ring.

"Huzzah! Huzzah!" he exclaimed as his courser pranced on its hind legs, then turned about in a circle, allowing him to address all members of the eager crowd. "Ladies and gentlemen, our thanks for honouring us with your company on this very fine afternoon! My friends and I will do everything in our power to gain your favour. Now, watch as we exhibit a variety of manly exercises with the horse, from the horse, and on the horse, the likes of which have never before been seen in the whole of England! Gibraltar, onward!"

Astley's steed reared even further, its hooves pawing the air, before stamping back to the dirt with a bang. Walk gave way almost immediately to canter, man and horse racing around the wide ring in a cloud of dust.

Belle's heart raced nearly as fast as Astley's steed. What joy, to ride with such uninhibited freedom and speed…

Patty's husband gradually slowed his horse and returned to the center of the ring. "We will now demonstrate the various airs of the *manége*, which those of you who wish to study military horsemanship may learn here at our school. Rye, to me! Gibraltar, *pesade*!"

Belle nearly jumped to her feet at the sight of Captain Rye atop a stallion as black and sleek as the panther in the Tower menagerie. How could the captain be even more compelling on horseback than on solid ground?

The men in the crowd roared as the captain joined Astley in cantering about the ring. Every nerve in Belle's body urged her to roar, too, to jump up and shout out his name as if she were an unruly grounding in the pit of a theater. Only the thought of the peal her Regiment of Refinement would ring over her if she did kept her in her seat.

Pressing her lips tight, she grasped the wooden bench beneath her with both hands as Astley and Rye led their horses through a series of skilled leaps, turns, pirouettes, and other military movements, explaining each's utility on the field of battle as they went.

Belle's booted feet tapped the ground, silently urging the riders on. What skill and finesse they displayed!

"Surely you must acknowledge, ladies and gentlemen, that my friend and I have the privilege of riding two of the best-trained horses in his Majesty's Light Dragoons!" Astley declared as he and the captain slowed their animals and returned to the center of the ring.

Belle pressed her lips tight to contain her shout of agreement.

"I've witnessed similar displays of cavalry prowess at Horse Guards," Lord Mowbray, sitting behind her, sniffed. "Surely we've not come all the way across the river only for a performance we could just have easily seen at Whitehall?"

Belle could not agree. On those rare occasions when her parents allowed her and her brother to accompany them to town during the Season, the parade grounds had always been one of her favorite places to visit. But she'd seen no soldier there guide his mount with greater control, or finesse, than either Astley or Rye.

When the two men abruptly dismounted by the paling, Belle's hold on the bench loosened in disappointment. Had the show ended barely before it had begun?

But then Captain Rye stepped forward, his eye scanning the gathered spectators before coming to rest on her party. The roguish grin lighting his face was surely directed to the entire crowd, but Belle's toes tingled, as if it had been intended only for her.

"And now, ladies and gentlemen," the captain called, sweeping his hand in his friend's direction, "a display of Mr. Astley's new method of training horses for the road, field, and his majesty's service!"

Belle, afraid Aunt Elizabeth might notice if she stared at the captain rather than at the gentleman actually performing, forced herself to look away from Rye and his handsome steed. But even as she watched Mr. Astley direct his horse to kneel, and then to sit up like a lady's lapdog, something in her remained attuned to his fellow performer, watching, too, from inside the paling.

Belle laughed along with the crowd when Astley's mount fetched a hat from atop a stake at the far side of the ring and carried it back to him—as if the white steed were a puppy rather than a horse!

But alarm quickly displaced laughter when Astley and a remounted Rye began to canter, then bent backwards and hung from their saddles by only their knees. Surely they could not hold such a position for long without sliding off their horses?

But somehow, both not only remained mounted, but also swept first the feathers on their caps, and then the fingertips of both their hands, along the packed dirt of the Ride. Belle felt her eyes grow wide as she watched them scoop up several handkerchiefs the stableboy set by a paling. Even jaded Lord Mowbray could not contain a shout of appreciation when, riding toward the other end of the ring at full speed, each snatched up a tiny sixpence the boy had ostentatiously displayed to the audience and then set on the ground.

When the two finally raised themselves to a proper seat, Belle pressed a hand against her chest in relief. But that relief was short-lasted; within moments, Astley and Rye were twisting their reins about their saddles' cantles, kicking off their stirrups, and leaping with the grace of ballet dancers to stand atop their cantering horses' backs. Belle's heart leapt, too, right into her throat. Even more dangerous, standing atop a racing horse!

But the two men did more than simply remain upright. First Astley, and then Rye, stood on one leg, as if imitating Mercury in flight, racing around the ring as steady on one foot as they had on two. And then each threw their left leg over their right knee, as if they were seated on a chair instead of standing on the back of a horse, maintaining that difficult pose for a complete turn about the ring.

And when they began to caper—first, the steps of some kind of peasant dance, and then a more intricate hornpipe—Belle could not help but press her gloved knuckles against her mouth, struggling to contain the potent mix of admiration and alarm roiling her insides. Please, *please*, let them not fall!

Both, thank heavens, remained as steady as rocks, dancing and frolicking as their mounts raced faster and faster about the ring.

Even the dour Glenlyon let loose a bark of amazement when a third rider joined the pair. A rider standing atop not one horse, but two. A rider not in the uniform of a cavalry officer, but in a habit of brightest red, trained skirts trailing out behind her as she raced in pursuit of her fellows.

Patty?

Most of the audience jumped to its feet at the appearance of a female rider, whistling and stamping in approval. And when Patty and the two men began springing from one horse to the other like drops of water popping and sizzling against a hot griddle—oh, how could anyone remain unmoved by such a display? Belle sprung from the bench, too, clapping and clapping until her hands grew sore.

The three swept up glasses the stableboy had filled with wine then raised them high. "To Englishmen—and Englishwomen—who, for activity on horseback, can justly challenge the entire world!" Astley exclaimed. Then the three drank a toast, with as much ease as if they had been seated in a tavern rather than standing atop galloping horseflesh.

If only Belle had learned, she would have whistled in appreciation, too, as the gentleman behind them just had. Instead, she had to settle for cheering until her voice grew hoarse.

Patty, who had moved to stand atop a single horse, offered a pert curtsy then urged her mount to leap over the rope fence. Captain Rye and her second mount quickly followed. Aunt Elizabeth pressed her hands over her ears, the crowd's roar of applause thundered so. But Belle didn't mind the noise in the least. How could she, when her blood sang in her veins at the glories of her friend's—and her friend's friend's—performance?

Even her aunt's wince could not keep Belle from cheering as loudly as the men as Astley cantered to the center of the ring, turning his horse in a complete circle as if it were dancing a minuet.

"Our thanks to you, ladies and gentlemen, for attending our performance this evening," he exclaimed over the huzzahing of the crowd. "Surely you must agree that never before was such an exhibition of horsemanship, and of such variety, seen in all of the whole of England. And all for the price of one shilling, not a tenth of the part of the value of such an extraordinary performance! Tell all your friends and relations that we welcome guests every evening, with doors opening at five, and the performance at six! And now, my fellow countrymen, I bid you good night!"

At his words, enthusiastic members of the audience rained appreciative coins down on the dirt ring. Lord Mowbry and Sir Frances left their seats to join the gentlemen pressing close to the rope ring to toss their own tributes. Astley moved closer to the crowd, cheering whenever a spectator managed to loft a shilling or sixpence directly into his proffered hat.

"Oh, did you ever see anything so exhilarating in your entire life?" Belle exclaimed to her aunt. "I simply must offer my congratulations to Patty."

And if a certain Captain Rye just happened to be nearby…

Well, Belle would never be so rude as to complain.

"Wait, my dear! Your uncle and I will accompany you! Just let me gather my belongings—"

Belle tapped a restless foot while Aunt Elizabeth searched for reticule and shawl. But she could not contain her impatience when a fellow Scot hailed her uncle just as they left the spectators' shed.

Before Aunt Elizabeth could forbid her, Belle slipped into the flow of the crowd. She followed it as far as the stables, then broke free to lift the door's latch and slip inside.

The scent of hay and sweaty horses, the sound of neighs and snorts and stamping hooves, the heat given off by animals far greater than a measly human—she touched a hand against the rough wood of a stall, taken aback by the familiarity of it all. When had she last spent any time in a stable? Not since her parents' death, no doubt. She had almost forgotten what a pleasure it could be, the quiet camaraderie of the stables, the calming, repetitive rhythm of French brush against warm, rippling horseflesh.

How she missed it! But unlike her father, none of her guardians thought it appropriate for a young lady to groom her own mount...

"Help you, miss?" A wizened groom tapped a curry comb against the top of a stall further down the row, his expression half curiosity, half askance.

Belle's hands curled in her gloves, resisting the ridiculous urge to snatch the comb from his gnarled fingers and set to grooming the horse beside him—one of the two Patty had ridden in the show—herself.

"Mrs. Astley. Where might I find her?"

"Along about back," the groom answered with a tilt of his head. "Ollie, take the lady back."

Belle nodded her thanks, then followed the stableboy deeper into the barn. She passed several boys hard at work cleaning tack and distributing fresh hay to the hungry inhabitants before reaching the stable's back door. Outside again, she found Patty beside a watering trough, encouraging her second horse to drink deep.

"Belle!" A proud smile lit her friend's elfin features. "Was it not a treat, today's performance? What my husband and Captain Rye can do—"

Belle shook her head, then gave Patty a half-embrace, half-shake. "What *they* can do? What of what *you* can do? When I think of all those times back at school when we argued over who was the better rider! Why did you never tell me how truly skilled you are?"

Patty laughed as her horse shook its head, spraying drops of water over them both. "Because what you saw today, I couldn't do any of it, not then. Not before I met Philip and Rye. They've both been so encouraging, both taught me so much—"

"As if you needed any encouraging to jump atop any animal, you harum-scarum creature!"

Even without turning, Belle knew immediately who had spoken the words, who had accompanied them with a low laugh. Because that laugh reverberated straight through her, clear down to the toes curling in her boots.

"If perchance a zebra, or a tapir, or even a rhinoceros, should find itself in your yard, it had best look sharp," the voice averred. "For audacious Patty Astley would simply climb right aboard!"

Something deep inside Belle sparked to life at the humor and affection in that deep voice. As if that humor and affection were directed at her, rather than at her friend…

She whirled to find the man she'd been admiring throughout the entire performance atop a different horse than the one he'd been riding earlier. He must have seen to that other horse first, though; rolled-up shirtsleeves and damp hair gave him a disheveled, almost reckless appearance.

Oh, how scandalous her Tutting Trustees would find the man's lack of propriety, speaking to a lady in such a state of undress.

Belle's breath caught, not in shock but in wonder at the barely contained energy shining from his crinkling green eyes. How spirit-stirring, the pride he must feel after such a performance! How thrilling, the wild acclaimed with which it had been greeted…

She turned away before he could catch sight of the admiration that must be burning in her own eyes.

Only to discover Patty with exaggeratedly raised eyebrows and a provokingly wriggling nose, casting significant glances between herself and the captain.

Oh, good heavens, she could *not* fall into a fit of the giggles, not now…

"Captain Rye," she said as she turned her back on her provoking friend and acknowledged the gentleman with a quick curtsey. "What an admirable performance, from all of you. How proud your family must be!"

Belle flinched as the warmth of his smile cooled. She'd been so flustered by his appearance, she'd forgotten that he'd not only lost his parents but also felt burdened by the weighty expectations of a grandfather and a brother, too.

"What need have we of familial approbation, when we'll soon have the whole of London at our feet?" Patty exclaimed. "Particularly when we add other acts—jugglers and clowns and acrobats—to fill the time between our riding demonstrations. If spectators keep flocking to our performances as they did today, Astley and I will soon have funds enough for expansion."

"Enough to employ every conjuror, rope dancer, and balance-master in Europe!" Captain Rye exclaimed, quickly shaking off whatever melancholy Belle's ill-considered comment had caused.

"And build a fine grandstand to boot!" Patty added.

"Astley's Grand Amphitheatre, the toast of the town!" Rye raised an invisible wine glass.

"Say rather, toast of the entire world!" Patty cried, leaning forward to clink her own imaginary glass against his.

Belle sighed. "Oh, how envious you make me! If only I could join you—"

She raised a hand to her mouth, shocked by her own words. Where had such an outlandish idea come from?

"What an unlikely desire for a lady of rank," Captain Rye said with a raised eyebrow.

Did that eyebrow convey admiration? Or doubt?

"Ah, but my friend comes from a long line of courageous ladies, do you not, Belle?" Patty exclaimed, quickly coming to her defense. "I still remember all the stories you told of your many audacious ancestresses."

"A real baroness performing at Astley's British Riding School?" The captain's eyes lit with unholy amusement. "Oh, what heights of puffery such a performer would inspire! I can hear Philip even now: 'Come one, come all, and witness the never-before-seen feats of the Flying Contessa, defying death atop her horse at every turn!'"

"'Watch as she conducts her toilette, takes her tea, and inspects her jewels, all while riding circles about the ring!'" Patty added.

"'Admire her skill as she dances a gavotte, a minuet, even a gigue, all atop her noble steed!'" Belle swept out an arm, then curtseyed, as if she were actually receiving accolades for such a performance.

Rye's horse lowered its head and gave her a friendly snuffle. Searching for a treat of some sort, the bold fellow.

Patty nudged a bit of apple into her hand.

Belle took off her glove, placed the treat in the middle of her open palm, then raised her hand to the horse's mouth. The tickle of its soft, velvety lips and the tiny whiskers about its mouth, as well as the approval in a gentleman's eyes as she spoiled his steed —such easy, simple pleasures they were. Yet sweeter, somehow, when shared with Captain Rye…

Belle replaced her glove, then offered her co-conspirators a wry smile. "If only I could claim such equestrienne skills. But I fear any performance of mine would turn away, rather than entice, the public."

"Don't be so modest, Belle! You always were a quick study." Patty laid a hand against the captain's boot. "I'd warrant Rye here could teach you in a trice."

"Indeed," the captain agreed. "Shall we give it a try?"

And without even waiting for her answer, he leaned over, set two large palms about her waist, and with seemingly effortless grace, set her right in front of him atop his horse.

Before she could offer the least protest—not that anyone could have heard it, not with Patty clapping and squealing in such clear delight—he kneed his horse into a brisk walk.

"Captain! You can't—you shouldn't! To snatch up a lady and ride off with her without even a by-your-leave! Oh, it is most improper…"

Outrage at such high-handed behavior ought to have infused every word of that protest. But she could hear little indignation, nay, not even irritation or mere annoyance, in her tone. No, a chastisement which should have snapped like a whip instead had been whispered, whispered with breathless, barely contained anticipation. Cheeks flushing, breath catching at the unfamiliar feeling of a man's arm about her waist, a man's muscled thighs beneath her own—why, it almost felt like freedom, like flying, flying without wings, this momentary escape from her Council of Constant Constraint.

Or was the frisson of danger more from dallying with a gentleman of whose intentions she could not be entirely certain?

"From what I've heard from Patty, Lady Culmaily could use a little impropriety in her oh-so-buttoned-up life," the captain interrupted, not chastened in the least by her feeble attempt at reproof. "Or at least a few moments of pleasure."

Oh, how presumptuous, to speak of her, *to* her, in such a familiar, knowing way! If they'd been in a ballroom, she would have snapped the ribs of her fan against his arm in swift rebuke.

But she had no fan, only fingers clutched tight in the fine, smooth strands of his horse's mane.

"What if someone were to see us?" she gasped. If word of such improper behavior were to be called to the attention of the Committee on Privileges—or, even worse, to the queen or the king—

"No need to worry," the captain said with a chuckle. "No one can tell I've anyone before me, not with my back to the crowd. And if I know Patty, she'll send Astley to entertain My Lady's Leash-holders so you and his wife might indulge in a cozy chat."

A cozy chat? When she sat perched on the lap of a brazen officer, trotting off to goodness knew where?

Belle's eyes had been fixed so intently on her hands, on holding tight to the moving horse, she'd not looked up once to see in which direction they were heading.

"But where are you taking me? To the riding ring?" she asked, finally daring to lift her eyes. But rather than the stables and crowds and paddocks she'd expected, rolling fields and orchards blossoming with the first hints of fruit lay on each side of the narrow track.

Behind her, she felt him shake his head. "I thought you'd prefer not to have an audience for your first lesson. You *did* wish to learn to ride, did you not?"

The exaggerated innocence of his tone, its humor, its *challenge*—was he *laughing* at her?

She jerked upright, her shoulder crashing against his chest.

"Oomph!" he cried in exaggerated protest. Exaggerated it surely was, for her movement had not unsteadied him in the least from his secure seat atop the horse.

Belle's temper began to flare. "I assure you, Captain, I've been well trained in all the equestrian arts suitable for a lady."

"But you've never been taught to soar atop your mount as Patty has, swift as a star shooting across the sky," he said, ignoring yet another less-than-cutting attempt to depress his impertinence. "And you want to. Deny it all you wish, but I won't soon forget the longing in your voice, the yearning in those cognac-kissed eyes. Eyes that so dazzled me when I first caught sight of them on the Grand Staircase at St. James's…"

An unfamiliar heat, sharp, shocking, blazed over Belle's entire person. And what was this urge to tuck closer into his body, to stare up into his own eyes, kissed not with cognac but by the springtime green of bluebell and daffodil shoots just emerging from the bracken? Oh, what a dangerous, dangerous man, to make her feel so, so—she hardly had the words to describe it, so unfamiliar were the desires he inspired.

But even the sense of danger he posed could not keep her decorously silent. "You truly think to teach me how to stand atop this beast?" she asked.

"Beast? Ah, you insult my poor Bellerophon. He may look fierce, but he's the gentlest creature imaginable, I assure you."

"Your horse is named *Belle*—Bellerophon?"

He laughed again, the sound humming against her ear. "*Arabella*, meet *Belle*rophon. A sign, is it not, the similarity of your names?"

"A sign of what?"

"That you and he—and you and I, perhaps?—are destined to become friends."

She had only meant to shoot the swiftest glance over her shoulder, just to check if he were making fun of her. But once she caught sight of that grinning, mobile mouth, those bright eyes alight with wicked humor, she found she couldn't look away.

And then he rose out of the saddle, pressing his body forward. His arm tightening about her waist. His mouth, only inches from hers…

Belle's breath caught. Was he going to—

Beneath her, Bellerophon surged, leaping from a walk directly into a canter. Her eyes shot forward, all silly expectation crashing back to the ground alongside the horse's hooves.

But disappointment immediately gave way to pleasure, and then to sheer exhilaration, as the wind rushed past her cheeks and her heartbeat pounded to the cadence of Bellerophon's hooves. The thrill of speed, of rocking in concert with the horse beneath her, of racing without hindrance or restraint—even when the wind sent her jockey-cap flying right from her head, Belle could not bring herself to complain.

Behind her, Captain Rye sat back in the saddle. When she cast him a reproving glance, the scoundrel only grinned.

It took genuine effort not to grin right back. Or to scold him when he pulled the reins into a half-halt, urging Bellerophon to slow. Oh, how she wanted to keep flying…

When the horse transitioned into a steady walk, Belle tossed her head, then patted the animal beneath her. "What a strong, brave horse you are! I would be pleased to stand such a fellow friend. Heavens knows you must be in need of one, what with such a reckless excuse for a master as Captain Rye."

"Reckless?" His tone suddenly hardened. "My brother and grandfather may call me madcap, but I'm never foolhardy or rash, I assure you. Particularly not when it comes to the well-being of those entrusted to my care."

Entrusted to his care… What would it be like to be so-entrusted?

Belle frowned, her hands tightening in Bellerophon's mane. She'd spent the last six years chafing at the kindly but officious care of not one but five male guardians. She should have felt just as restricted, just as constrained, by this man, too, a man who presumed to wrap powerful arms and protective words about a lady whom he'd just met.

Why, then, did her mind slip straight to the words *precious*, and *cherished*, instead?

Belle's jaw clenched. Foolish, foolish girl! A married woman such as Patty might admire a heedless jackanapes with little consequence, but Lady Culmaily could hardly do the same….

Rye wheeled about the edge of an orchard redolent with the scent of ripening plums, pulling his horse to a halt beside an open field. In its center, tall green summer grasses waved in the late afternoon breeze, the scarlet of poppies, the purples of cornflowers and vetch, the creams of daisies and meadowsweet and clover, rippling beside them. Around its edges lay a wide swath of stamped-down turf, impressed with the occasional mark of a horse's hoof.

"I often come here when I wish to try out a new trick far from prying eyes," Rye explained. "Embarrassing to have an audience whistling and catcalling at every inevitable misstep."

And then he was wrapping the reins around a low tree branch, shimmying out from behind her, and sliding off Bellerophon's backside, just as he had during the earlier performance.

Leaving her alone atop his frighteningly powerful steed…

Out of instinct, Belle grabbed for the reins, but then slowly drew her fingers back and wove them once again in the horse's mane, holding the rest of her body perfectly still. Who knew to what commands an animal trained in such unusual feats of horsemanship would answer?

"Ready for your lesson?" he asked as he moved to stand beside his horse's head. "Or shall we turn around and go back?"

She'd never imagined how a single cocked brow could convey such mockery, or such challenge.

Belle's jaw set, and she gave a curt nod. "I am ready."

He nodded in return, then took up the reins in one hand. "First, take hold of the pommel with your left hand." With a gentleness she'd not been expecting, he used his free hand to unravel her fingers from his horse's mane and set them on the front of the saddle.

Her entire person thrilled, not just at his touch, but at the matter-of-fact confidence of his tone. He truly thought her capable of doing what he and Patty had done? She, Arabella Audley? A lady whom a plethora of guardians did not think able of making a single decision, never mind doing something as daring as stand atop a horse—

Well, if he thought her able, she'd not allow her own fears, nor the anticipation of the peals her guardians would all ring over her for such a heedless act, to keep her from proving him right.

She drew in a deep breath as her fingers curved around the pommel.

The delight in his sudden, winsome smile—why, she'd risk far more than simply clutching at a saddle to inspire such a response again.

"Now, lean to the right, then swing your left knee so that it rests atop the saddle."

Belle leaned and swung, but not, it seemed, quite in the way he'd intended.

"No, keep your right leg extended," Rye corrected. "Here, I'll move your skirts out of the way."

Belle's breath caught as Rye took hold of her riding dress and carefully tugged her tangled skirt and petticoats free. Just imagine the paroxysms of outrage both Lady Mowbray and Lady Kerr would have fallen into at such a sight!

But there was nothing presuming or lascivious about his touch. Only the touch of a teacher, correcting a misguided student.

Belle looked quickly away, fearing her face might reveal her utterly inappropriate sense of disappointment at the fact.

"Now, set your other boot *behind* the saddle, atop Bellerophon's loin."

She raised her foot and set it where he had instructed, clutching at the pommel as she rose into an awkward squat. She wobbled and tilted, her innards quenching tight until at last she finally found her balance. *Steady on, steady on…*

"Yes, just like that!" Rye exclaimed, his voice deepening in encouragement. "Now, bend your knees as you rise from your crouch."

Rise from her crouch? Belle shot him an incredulous look. As if she weren't in danger of toppling completely from Bellerophon's back as it was!

But Rye only offered her a cheeky wink.

She jerked her eyes from his, only to find them fixing on the ground. The ground so very far below her…

Belle swallowed.

"Slowly, *slowly*, you don't wish to spook him," Rye instructed.

Slowly? As if she had been moving at all!

She didn't know how long she'd crouched, unmoving, before she felt his hand rest gently against hers. Hands clutched tighter to the pommel than a barnacle to a ship.

"You can do it, my lady," he said. "I'm certain of it."

His hand gave hers a light squeeze, then gradually pulled away, leaving her free to choose. To choose the doubt and distrust of her least self. Or the confidence and courage of her best.

Belle set a palm flat against Bellerophon's crest and pushed.

"Yes!" Rye exclaimed, excitement rippling like a ribbon through his voice. "There you are!"

And yes, there she was, looking down from a height she'd never imagined, standing astride the mighty beast.

How different the world looked from such a height, and from such a glory of accomplishment…

She could not help but laugh, laugh at the joy, the sheer exhilaration of the power of directing, even for just a moment, her own self. At the pleasure of, for once, being able to exercise her own will.

Below her, Rye laughed, too, pride clearly animating his wonderfully expressive face. Pride not just in his own accomplishment in teaching, but in hers at daring to be taught.

"Steady?" he asked.

The eagerness of her nod threw her a bit off balance, sending her arms windmilling awkwardly through the air. But instead of crying out, she laughed again, near giddy from the potent mix of amusement and alarm.

He chuckled, too, even as he set a strong, steadying hand against her boot. Laughing at her a bit, but even more *with* her, at the ridiculousness of a baroness standing atop a horse, at the gorgeousness of the summer afternoon, at the sheer joy of taking an unexpected risk. *Do not be afraid to try*, that warm, reassuring grip seemed to say. *I'll be here to catch you should you fall…*

When had she last laughed so much she could barely catch her breath?

She suddenly remembered John, before he grew ill, chasing her down Audley Priory's oak tree-lined avenue. She'd felt teased and tormented, then, too, but also thrilled to find herself the center of her older brother's attention as she swerved off the track and across the bowling green, skittered precariously close to the edge of the ha-ha, startling the deer below with her cry as he came within inches of catching her.

Yes, it felt like that, that restless, giddy mixture of excitement and pleasure and fear, lording it over the entire world from atop a towering, magnipotent horse.

But not *exactly* like that, not precisely, no. Because it was a man's, not a boy's, eyes that were fixed upon her now.

And because the feelings spiraling around her insides when she looked at that man felt nothing in the least fraternal…

She slid down to Bellerophon's back with a groan. *Feelings!* She had no time to attend to anything as trivial as feelings. No, all her thoughts should be on Audley Priory, on her plan for regaining her father's title for herself and his—her—heirs.

"Enough?" he asked.

Belle gave a weary nod, wiping a gloved hand against her damp brow. "I don't suppose there's a nearby burn from which we might steal a sip?"

"No beck nor brook, alas," Rye said. But his eyes, and smile, held nothing of disappointment. "What would you say to something far more refreshing?"

Strong arms reached up to grasp her waist and swing her down from the horse. Belle choked back a gasp, feeling almost as if she'd had the wind knocked clear out of her at the touch of his confident hands against her sides, the brush of his curls against her cheek.…

Seemingly unaware of the near-bewildering effect his touch had on her, he grabbed her hand and pulled her with boyish excitement through clumps of oxeye daisies toward a stand of trees by the field's edge. Humming an unfamiliar tune, he bent, nudging aside leafy debris and straw to reveal a clump of low-lying toothed-edged leaflets, a handful of delicate white flowers standing in their midst. And beneath those leaves, curved stems, arched, eager, offering elongated, conical fruits, some still white, some turning green, some the rubiest of reds, all smaller than the tiniest of her brother's marbles—

"Strawberries!" she exclaimed. "'Fruit from heaven,' my mother used to call them. 'A gift from the hand of God'."

"'Aphrodite's tears,' my father always said." Rye's eyes crinkled in memory. "Because after the goddess's lover Adonis was gored to death by a boar, her falling tears mixed with his blood, then transformed into heart-shaped berries. Or so an ancient Italian he met during his Grand Tour once told him."

"Oh, one of my father's favorite lines from Virgil was about strawberries! *Qui legatos flores et numi nascenti fraga, / frigidus, a pueri, fugite hinc, latent anguis in herba.*"

In response to Rye's inquisitive eyebrow, she translated: "'Ye who cull flowers and low-growing strawberries, Away from here lads; A chill snake lurks in the grass'."

"Ah, the dangerous strawberry! The risk one hazards by partaking of its pleasures."

"Or the risk that evil may lie hidden beneath its beauty."

Rye gave a rueful laugh, an odd sound from the mouth of such an apparently lighthearted man. "What strange things can bring the memory of a long-lost parent rushing back into one's mind."

"Yes," Belle agreed, her throat aching in sympathy for his loss, and in grief for her own. But somehow that familiar ache seemed lighter today, a wistful, loving longing rather than the sharp bite of sorrow.

Because he, like her, knew the same loss, felt the same grief?

Belle pulled off a glove and ran a finger against the surface of an unripe berry, the bumps of its seeds as rough as the heads of the pins pressed into her favorite pincushion. "Such a tiny thing to bear the weight of so many different meanings," she offered, trying to break the unsettling moment of unexpected commiseration.

But Rye's hand, ungloved as well, brushed against her bare fingers once, then again, in affinity. Affinity all the more powerful for its silence.

When she looked down at it, she saw he held a fully ripened berry between thumb and forefinger. She glanced up at his face, expecting to find a teasing grin, but instead saw the same intense expression he'd worn when he first set eyes on her at St. James's.

He offered her the ruddy fruit, bypassing her extended palm to hold it just out of reach of her lips.

Her shockingly eager lips.

Her cheeks strawberrying at her own daring, she raised her hand and drew his towards her mouth. Her lips kissing against his fingers, her teeth caught the ripened berry and pulled it into her mouth.

The flare of its flavors—sweet but tart, vanilla and rose and violet—seasoned by the salt of his skin, burst like a banquet over the buds of her tongue.

The sudden flare of light in his eyes—oh, how it hinted of even deeper, richer pleasures…

"'*Where are you going, pretty maid, with your white face and your yellow hair?' / 'I'm going to the spring, kind sir, for strawberry leaves make maidens fair,*'" he sang to the tune he'd been humming a few moments before. "I never did understand, though, why any girl would choose to chew on strawberry leaves if the lusciousness of its fruit were to hand. Especially a girl already the fairest of the fair. How very lovely you are, my dearest, darling Arabella—"

He moved closer, closer, as if compelled to partake of the pleasure of the fruit by way of her lips—

Strawberry leaves?

Before those ripe lips could touch hers, those words jerked her back.

Strawberry leaves on her court dress. Eight strawberry leaves on the coronet of an earl—

Belle swallowed, a stray seed catching, scratching in her throat. What in heaven's name was she doing, flirting like a wanton with a gentleman who could never help her regain the Audley earldom?

She took a step back, then another, a hand pressing against her mother's brooch. Thank heavens she'd not lost it during this ill-considered lesson.

"I thank you, Captain, for your instruction. This day will serve as a cherished memory of freedom once I am married. But I must return to the riding school, without delay!"

"Married?" Captain Rye's eyes narrowed. "Are you betrothed, then, my lady?"

Belle whirled and dashed across the field, daises crushing beneath her retreating feel. How could she have spent so much time alone with this man, a man she barely knew?

A man who could never help her realize her dreams…

"No," Belle threw over her shoulder, then scoured the edge of the field for the path back to the school. "But I will be," she said, as much to herself as to him. "I must be, and without delay, if I am to regain my father's title."

Ah, there, just behind a stand of white birches—

She increased her pace, dismayed at how unthinking she'd allowed herself to be. Poor Aunt Elizabeth must be near mad with worry—

"If you'll just wait a moment while I untie Bellerophon, I'll walk you back," he called from behind her. "Are you not already Lady Culmaily?"

"A Scottish baroness, yes," she answered, but did not slow. "A title which I inherited in my own right. But my father also held a second title, an English earldom, which cannot pass to a daughter."

"An earldom, as well as a barony?"

Was it a pebble, or the sharpness of his words, that nearly made her stumble? She threw a quick glance over her shoulder and saw him rushing to catch her up, his forehead beneath a stray lock of tawny hair—oh, why should she find such a ridiculous feature so attractive?—wrinkling in confusion.

"Yes," she said, then kicked at a stone blocking her path.

"And I must marry one of the men currently laying claim to that earldom if I am to ensure it continues in his direct line."

"A contested title?" The sound of Rye's footsteps, as well as Bellerophon's, came to an abrupt halt. "To what earldom do you refer?"

"My father was the Earl of Audley." And then, without allowing him a moment to question, or protest, or to sweep her up again and set her atop his horse, Belle yanked up her skirts and raced back down the narrow track from which they had come. Back towards the stables and the paddock and her aunt and great uncle and guardians. The Keepers of her Gilded Cage.

Back to her duty.

Disappointment, embarrassment at no horse's hooves pounding in swift pursuit, no arm sliding about her waist and lifting her into a warm lap, made tears prick at the corners of her eyes.

But then—

"Lady Culmaily! Arabella! Wait, let me escort you back—"

Belle stumbled at his words, at the sight of her abandoned jockey-cap caught on the branch of a tree. She jerked the cap free, then took up her skirts again and raced even faster down the path. Ridiculous, pointless, unwelcome, such maudlin feelings! And for a man practically a stranger?

Her lips pressing tight, she forced her yearning—for his laughter, for the passion he promised, for the companionship her parents had shared, both like-minded lovers and friends— down, down, down deep.

She would not look back.

THE ROYAL BIRTHDAY BALL

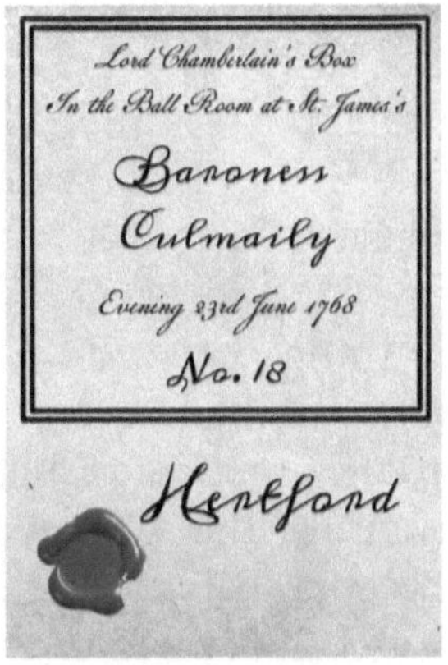

"Oh, what a crush! I knew we should have left earlier. Now we'll be reduced to sitting at the very back of the chaperone's box, and no one of any consequence will take the least note of us at all! What an unfortunate turn of affairs…"

Lady Mowbray's fretful words contained no overt chastisement. But Belle had become all too familiar with those pursed lips, the fingers tight with tension as they fussed at Belle's coiffure and the fussy furbelows on her court gown. The earl's wife blamed Belle for their late return to St. James's for the most important event of the day: the King's Birthday Ball.

What had Arabella been thinking, the lady's pinched expression seemed to say, *to dally so long at a low entertainment when she had a far more important event for which to prepare?*

Belle grimaced at the thought of what the lady might say if she knew not what, but who, had kept her dallying…

"Loop your train over your arm, so that others cannot tread on it!" Lady Kerr counseled as she scrutinized the crowd milling about the west end courtyard of the palace.

Belle searched the crowd, too. And if her insides soared as high as a gyrfalcon at the sight of every scarlet-clad back, then thumped disappointingly back to earth when each turned out not to be the one for which her wayward eyes searched… Well, no one but she would be the wiser.

"Damned foolish, such old-fashioned court dress," Uncle Andrew muttered, yanking the small sword hanging at his side away from Belle's voluminous skirts. "Can't understand why the king insists on keeping to the old ways."

"Ignorant of anything beyond your own provincial standards," Lord Mowbray sniffed as they hurried with the rest of the late arrivals from the outer court through the ground-floor passage at the south end of the Chapel Royal. "Every *English* gentleman knows that Louis XIV despised the informal loose gowns that came into style at the end of the last century, and so mandated ladies wear *robes de court* at all formal events."

"And your monarchs follow his example?" Sir Alexander asked. "How droll, to see them aping a ghost of French fashion while simultaneously congratulating themselves on their superior English taste."

"A great admirer of feminine shoulders and décollaté, the Sun King," Sir Francis interposed, cutting off Sir Alexander's impending peroration on English hypocrisy before he could offend anyone in the crowd. "Perhaps our monarch shares his preferences?"

Someone bumped into Belle from behind, causing one of her wide whalebone hoops to bounce.

"Oh, I do beg your pardon, ma'am. Please excuse my

clumsiness!" A very young gentleman, all gangly shuffling feet and flailing hands, flapped an apology in Belle's direction.

"And here I thought hoops were designed expressly to keep unwanted fellows at a distance," Sir Francis quipped.

The young gentleman's rounded cheeks flushed painfully red. And before Belle could even acknowledge his apology—or, perhaps more to the point, Sir Francis bedevil him further—he bowed, turned, and fled into the crowd.

"For heaven's sake, Thurlow," Lady Mowbray chastised Sir Francis with a frown. "That was one of Bute's sons! Do you mean to offend the king's closest advisor?"

"Ah, but how is an Englishman to tell one young Scot from the next?" Sir Alexander said, the sarcastic wave of his arm sending Belle's hoops a-bounce yet again.

"Set a hand on your hoop; that will keep it still," Lady Mowbray advised, even as she shot Sir Alexander a quelling look.

"Oh, but take care not to allow them to ride up and show your chemise!" Lady Kerr nearly moaned.

Sir Francis chuckled. "Yes, take care Arabella! For, as the poet warns, 'A hoop eight yards wide / May decently show your garters are tied.'"

Not just a wide hoop, Belle thought, her cheeks coloring. Twisting and turning atop Bellerophon had undoubtedly given Captain Rye more than a sight of her garters.

"Enough, Francis," Glenlyon said, shooting him a quelling glare as the party began its ascent up a staircase, one far narrower than the one upon which they'd waited this morning. At its top stood not the Guard Room, but a short Tudor gallery, which in turn opened to the largest room in the palace: the ballroom built by Christopher Wren for Queen Anne just before the turn of the last century.

Inside, Belle could see a railing which divided the place for dancing from the rest of the room. Benches for the chaperones and a gallery for spectators behind them lined both long walls. A small group of musicians sat at the ready in another gallery at the opposite end of the room.

Glenlyon flourished their tickets—the ones granting him and their party entrance to the chaperone's boxes, as well as the one bestowing Belle entrance to the Lord Chamberlain's box, where those who had applied to dance would wait their turn— and the yeoman guard bowed them in.

Belle's eyes roved as Glenlyon led their party into the ballroom. Even though she'd only been introduced to London society for the first time a week earlier, Glenlyon had drilled her for days beforehand so that she'd recognize the names of aristocrats with whom she would be expected to take her rightful place. Time well spent, for now she could put more than a few faces to those names, especially those gentlemen her guardians deemed most influential in advancing her cause.

Her Ducks of Decorum would certainly not consider a mere captain in His Majesty's Royal Regiment of Light Dragoons among their number. Nor should she. But something contrary inside her sent her eye roving over the crowds, wondering, hoping…

"For whom are you searching with such particular attention, my dear?" Aunt Elizabeth asked, her voice both kind and knowing.

Belle bit her lip and pressed her left ankle to the top of her right foot. Lady Mowbray had insisted that pearls were the only jewels a lady making her debut at court could possibly wear. But Belle couldn't face such a vitally important event without a token of her family's love close to hand. So she'd circumvented her worrisome guardian's restriction by threading her mother's heart brooch onto the ribbon of her dancing slipper when the lady had been distracted by yet another tedious tiff with Lady Kerr. The prick of the edge of the brooch served as a much-needed reminder to act with greater discretion.

"The gentleman with whom I am to dance this evening," she offered, feeling her cheeks color at the half-truth. "If only I knew who he was…"

Aunt Elizabeth shook her head. "If only it could be Glenlyon, or Mowbray, or any other partner of your choosing!"

"Or more to the point, *their* choosing," Belle said with a wry smile. "How they all must be chafing at the convention of a royal birthday ball, requiring that dancers be paired in strict order of precedence. Whom do you think will open the dancing?"

"I believe the king's brother, the Duke of Gloucester, is the highest-ranking gentleman after the king in attendance tonight," Aunt Elizabeth answered. "He'll lead out the Duchess of Northumberland, and perhaps the Duchess of Marlborough, too, if she is not *enceinte* yet again. Or perhaps the Countess of Rothes, who was just lately married?"

"We could count down the gentleman in order of precedence to try and discover your partner," Lady Mowbray said.

"A vain effort, I fear," Sir Francis warned. "Most of the gentleman are here to talk politics, not tread a measure. The ones who have volunteered are so few, they must dance with not one partner but two, I understand."

"I told you we should have all submitted our names," Lord Mowbray scolded. "Far better if Lady Culmaily stood up with one of us than a gentleman unknown to her."

Sir Francis chuckled. "With you, Mowbray? When everyone knows you're as graceless as a cow?"

Belle ignored the Squabbling Squadron to examine her ticket, upon which a large "No. 18" had been scrawled in the Lord Chamberlain's hand. What gentleman had the matching number on his?

"I only hope that whoever he is, he will be a gentleman of some grace," Lady Elizabeth whispered. "I fear it won't be easy to follow a partner with whom you have never danced."

"How awful, to become the subject of amusement or ridicule for the entire court!" Lady Kerr shuddered.

"Not only court, but for the general public, too," Lady Mowbray said with no little relish. "Do you recall, Elizabeth, several seasons back, when Colonel Northvale stepped on the king's toes and almost tumbled into the lap of majesty? And how the newspapers ridiculed him in the days that followed?"

"Newspapers?" Belle asked, raising a hand in search of her mother's brooch. But her gloved fingers found only pearls.

"Be not fashed, lambie," Aunt Elizabeth whispered. "As long as you regulate your emotions and do not succumb to an affective display, all will be well."

Oh, if only she could be partnered by Captain Rye! His ease and grace atop a horse surely must translate to an equal elegance in the dance. And those teasing eyes would certainly make her smile, and laugh, and forget about the intense scrutiny of the *ton*...

"Here we are, ladies," Glenlyon said, jerking her free of the unwelcome thought. Her oldest chaperone indicated a length of empty bench toward the back of one of the chaperones' boxes.

"Just as I feared," Lady Mowbray fretted. "Not the least chance of any royal notice from here."

Belle was happy to leave the rest of their party to soothe the ruffled countess and follow Glenlyon toward the railing set off for the dancing.

"Hertford," Glenlyon greeted the Lord Chamberlain when they reached his box. "Here is Lady Culmaily, come to wait her turn to dance. But we do not know with whom she is partnered."

Lord Hertford, the Chamberlain's white wand of office in one hand, glanced down at what appeared to be a list of the night's dancers' in his other. But before he could find her name, the musicians began to play the march from Handel's *Judas Maccabeus*, and the yeomen guarding the barrier that enclosed the space reserved for dancing rushed off. The Lord Chamberlain nodded a quick apology then followed, signaling that the doors to the ballroom should be closed.

Glenlyon grimaced. "I'll try to discover with whom you're partnered. While I do, take care to watch the dancers, and model your own movements after theirs. And when it comes your turn, do not forget to comport yourself with grace and ease. Having the newspapers number you as one of the ladies who most excel at the dance cannot but help our cause with the king."

Belle pressed damp gloves against her hoops as the monarchs entered from opposite ends of the ballroom and began to bestow notice and approbation on the waiting dancers. Both offered Belle a nod before expeditiously moving on to the next couple in the circle.

And then the king and queen were taking their seats, and the Earl of Hertford bowed to the king's brother, his royal highness, the Duke of Gloucester, and to the Duchess of Northumberland, just as Aunt Elizabeth had surmised. Belle carefully observed the way each made their obeisances to the king and queen, then retired backwards ("One never turns one's back upon the monarchs!") until they arrived at the opposite end of the open space. The court dancing-master then spread the duchess's long, heavy train as the musicians struck up a minuet.

Belle marveled at the duchess's genteel deportment—her languid eye, smiling mouth, unaffected hands—as she traversed the floor, looking as if the obtrusive train of her robe à la française were merely an extension of her own person. Had she, like Belle, practiced dancing for hours with her hoop covered in a tablecloth, the elaborate court dress and train far too valuable to risk wearing for a mere rehearsal?

"Lady Culmaily," a voice from behind her quavered. "We are both in luck this evening, it would appear."

Audley Seagrave, one hand on his cane, the other clutching

the railing beside her, offered her a genial nod.

Belle started. How had she forgotten that the elder Seagrave meant to introduce her to his grandson this evening?

"Are we, sir? In what regard?"

"In regards to your dancing partner. I understand from Glenlyon that you hold the number eighteen."

"I do indeed, sir," Belle answered, surprisingly cheered by the sight of the old man. A schemer, just like herself....

She offered him her sauciest smile, a smile he returned with an appreciative wink.

"Then you are to tread a measure with my eldest grandson and namesake, Mr. Aubrey Seagrave, who holds both numbers seventeen and eighteen. Aubrey, make your bows to Lady Culmaily."

As she caught sight of the younger gentleman, the entire ballroom seemed to brighten, as if dozens of chandeliers had suddenly descended from the ceiling to gild the lackluster gathering.

Rye?

But just as quickly, gloom returned, the false rush of recognition displaced by dull disappointment. For while the gentleman beside Sir Aubrey may have stood just as tall as Captain Rye, may have been just as broad in shoulder and back, may have even shared the same tawny hair, his eyes were brown, not green, and he wore no red coat. Even more telling, his expression displayed none of the warm animation that so-enlivened the Captain's.

Despite his cool countenance, the younger Seagrave made her an elegant leg. "Your servant, ma'am."

Belle curtsied, taking care her wide hoops did not bounce as she lowered and rose. "And yours, sir."

"As I told you this morning, gel, I've no wish to take on the burdens of a wife at my age," the elder Seagrave whispered in her ear, sending the feathers curving over her head a-flutter. "But if you were to wed my eldest grandson, here, my petition for the Audley title could be combined with yours. Do you not think such a joint request would be looked upon with favor by the king?"

The gleam of satisfaction in the older gentleman's eyes—an invitation to join his scheme, and to share his satisfaction in its prospects.

Marrying the Seagrave grandson would not *guarantee* she'd ever gain the title Countess of Audley—if her husband were to die before his grandfather, and she'd not yet given birth to a son, the title would pass to another relative after the elder man's death. But it would heighten the odds considerably.

And a socially acceptable path, marrying the younger Seagrave, even if his rank was decidedly below her own. A path she'd warrant would be far more welcome to conventional King George than granting a title to a young woman outright...

The older man, clearly responding to the flash of understanding in her eyes, jerked his head towards his grandson.

A relief, this unexpected chance to hold on to her father's title without having to wed an aged gentleman, or a noted fop. Or so it should have been. But her hands and shoulders only tightened as she inspected this potential *parti*. A handsome fellow, to be sure, but his expression of aloof reserve seemed to rime the very air about him. How had she ever mistaken him for the lively Captain Rye?

"I am pleased to know with whom I will be partnered for the dance, sir," she offered, forcing herself not to recoil from his chill. "May I enquire with which dancing master you trained?"

"I have made a study of the minuet with Gennaro Magri these several years," he replied, his chin rising to an alarming angle. "You need not worry that I will embarrass you, madam."

Belle blinked in surprise. The younger Seagrave may have made an extensive study of the dance, but appeared to have spent far less time devoting himself to the art of polite conversation. Was he always so quick to take umbrage?

She forced herself to counter his frown with a civil smile. "And I with Monsieur Denoyer. They teach the rhythm of the minuet in a similar manner, do they not? So we should have no difficulties matching our steps."

Her partner only offered the shortest of nods, then said not another word.

Belle pressed her lips tight. But she did not turn away in outright dismissal. Father had taught her that first impressions were not always correct. The gentleman might only be naturally reserved, or a bit shy. Or perhaps even embarrassed by being pressed into a courtship with a lady with whom he had not the least acquaintance.

"Come, come, Audley, have I taught you nothing?" His grandfather tapped his cane against the wooden floor. "You must do better than that! Compliment the chit's gown, tell her how lovely she looks, how the other ladies seem but winking stars by comparison to this glorious Diana! Your brother may be a brash, disobedient fellow, but he certainly knows how to charm a gel!"

"Sir, you well know I have no talent for cajoling blandishment," the younger man said, his lip curling in disdain. "Lady Culmaily will be better served knowing now that she will be marrying a direct, plain-speaking gentleman, rather than find herself deceived by false flattery after the fact."

"Then let me speak just as plainly, sir," Belle said, trying not to grind her teeth. "I have no interest in being flattered, especially by a potential husband. What I require is a clear understanding of his views on the proper management of an estate. Would you be so kind as to inform me of yours?"

His eyebrows rose. "Estate management? Of what concern should that be to a lady?"

"Don't be such a fool, Audley!" his grandfather chided. "The chit simply wishes to know you will not run her source of income into the ground, nor gamble it away from under her."

Turning his back on his grandson, he leaned closer to Belle. "I assure you, my lady, my grandson is no adventurer, not at the tables, nor in any other sort of hazardous enterprises."

"Not *this* grandson," the younger man exclaimed, as if she should be as familiar with, and as contemptuous of, another, far more reckless, and thus less deserving, Audley descendant than he.

"Careful, sirrah," his grandfather warned. "You would not wish Lady Culmaily to think that jealousy of a sibling indicates a propensity in your character to jealousy in general. Hardly an attractive trait in a spouse, that."

The younger Seagrave flushed, the first genuine show of emotion from him she'd seen. If they were to marry, perhaps she could help reconcile him with this wayward sibling?

His grandfather tapped the head of his cane sharply against the dance floor railing. "My lady, I've taught Seagrave well how to manage property. Especially the importance of not tolerating tenants to fall into arrears. You will never have cause to fear on that account."

"Nor that I will ever burden you with the details of such tedious business," the younger Seagrave assured her. "No wife should have to concern herself with the mundane matters of the world."

No wife *should*. But what if a wife *wished*?

Before she could form the words to inquire, the elder gentleman pressed his cane against his grandson's back, urging him towards the dance floor. "Couple sixteen is almost finished! Remember, the Lord Chamberlain will not announce you in advance, Audley. Go and pay your honors to the monarchs with your first partner, sirrah!"

Belle waved—no, *wafted*—her fan, watching the younger Seagrave and a lady unknown to her meet on the floor, make their bows and courtesies to each other, and then offer the same to the king and queen. The musicians struck up an unfamiliar tune, and the pair spiraled about one another in the first steps of the minuet.

"A competent, even graceful, dancer, is he not?" the older gentleman whispered.

"Indeed, sir," Belle whispered back from behind her fan.

She watched the younger man's arms moving in gentle, curving arcs as he swirled his partner.

She feared he would not accept her interest in running her father's estate with equal grace.

"He may not have the charm of his rogue of a brother," the elder Seagrave whispered as the musicians played the final measures of the minuet. "But do not dismiss him out of hand, my dear. A dutiful boy, and a loyal one, if one is lucky enough to win his regard."

As the minuet came to an end, M. Desnoys, not only Belle's private instructor but the court dancing master, too, appeared at her side. "May I, my lady?" he asked, nodding toward the train of her gown, which she had draped over her arm.

Belle nodded, in part to the dancing master, in part to Sir Audley, then swept toward the dance floor. M. Desnoys followed, spreading out her train behind her.

Audley Seagrave waited for her in the middle of the floor. Since he had already paid his respects to the king and queen with his previous partner, Belle had to make her royal obeisances alone. Her heart beat almost as rapidly as it had when she'd climbed atop Rye's horse as she knelt in her lowest curtsey—ouch, how her legs ached from this afternoon's adventures!—then backed carefully away.

Beside her, Audley Seagrave bowed and held out his hand. Forcing herself not to tremble, she curtsied, then set her own in his.

Plié, half coupée, fleuret, half coupée, bourée; forward, back, right, left, turning, turning, turning. Neck free and easy. Chest full and shoulders drawn well back. Arms and hands moving in gentle, curving arcs.

Sink and rise with a gentle, but commanding flexibility. Vary the expression of the face, but maintain a modest, expressive eye…

The litany of instructions offered by her Lords and Ladies of Lectures gradually faded as Belle fell into the rhythm of the dance, and of the gentleman with whom she was partnered. The young man had not lied when he'd asserted his dancing would not embarrass. Indeed, she was certain all the court would agree that he was one of the most elegant gentlemen to take the floor this evening.

But when she shared that opinion with him, he merely nodded. No polite pleasantries, no brief observations on the weather or the music or the gathering, not for him.

Did he believe true elegance demanded silence? Or was he simply a boor?

They danced the rest of the minuet without exchanging another word.

Belle suppressed the giddy urge to laugh as finally, blessedly, the musicians returned to the key in which they had begun, the final third of the minuet. This dismal trial by dance would soon be done!

But suddenly, as if overly-hasty relief had summoned misfortune, she felt a sharp tug against her ankle. And then felt her dancing slipper slide right off her toes—

Her eyes flew to the floor in horror. Her mother's brooch must have caught, somehow, on Audley Seagrave's shoe buckle. And now both her slipper and the brooch lay on the ballroom's parquet floor….

Chuckles, twitters, even outright guffaws swarmed in Belle's ears as both she and the musicians stumbled to an awkward stop.

Belle glancing toward Glenlyon and the rest of her

guardians. Curling lips, gaping mouths, slack jaws and white faces—she'd never imagined so many ways a person's expression might convey consternation and dismay.

She closed her eyes, imagining the caricatures in the newspapers, Lady Mowbray's aggrieved plaints, all hopes for the king's favor spiraling out of her grasp…

Oh, could someone incinerate from shame?

Audley Seagrave, at least, did not join in the general mirth. But neither did he come to her aid. How could he not realize her over-wide hoops and heavy brocade gown would never allow her to retrieve the errant slipper herself?

Suddenly another gentleman, his red coat gleaming in the candlelight, was bending to the floor beside her, scooping up her slipper in one gloved hand.

"Give that to me," Seagrave hissed down at the man's bent head, as if only just realizing his incivility in not retrieving it himself.

But her rescuer ignored the command, kneeling instead at Belle's feet.

And when the gentleman raised his head, and a pair of green eyes and a laughing face met hers, she could barely constrain her gasp.

Rye?

With what she knew must be an unsightly blush, Belle raised her skirts, just high enough to reveal a single stockinged toe. But the increasingly loud laughter of the court—even the queen gave a restrained titter—did not daunt her rescuer. No, Captain Rye just gave her a wink as he slipped a hand beneath the ruffle at her hem, slid the shoe back on her foot, and retied its errant ribbon.

Every nerve in her body thrilled as his fingers lingered, whispering silent caresses over the bones of her ankle, the unexpectedly sensitive top of her foot…

At some unseen signal, the musicians began to play once

again. Seagrave started, then turned his back on her and took up the dance again, leaving Belle to scramble to catch him up, with no chance to offer her thanks to the gallant captain.

Belle danced the final steps by rote, eyes smarting with embarrassment, and shame, and something far different than either, something wary but wakeful and wanting....

"What a mortifying display," her partner hissed when the music finally came to an end.

She blinked as tears pricked the corners of her eyes.

No! Scandalous, it would be, to add an unsightly affective display to what the Privy Council of Propriety and their wives were certain to deem an already highly disgraceful exhibition. She would not allow herself the relief of tears, not in front of the entire court. She *would not*.

She sank into her final curtsy before the monarchs. Queen Charlotte could not seem to bring herself to meet Belle's eyes, but King George was generous enough to offer her an encouraging smile.

"Ah, Lady Culmaily," the king exclaimed, his slightly protruding eyes a-twinkle. "If old King Edward had been your partner, he must have instituted the Honor of the Slipper rather than the Honor of the Garter! Alas, I cannot emulate Edward's example and place your slipper on my own foot."

The members of the court laughed at the king's wit in invoking the apocryphal story of the founding of the Order of the Garter.

"Perhaps, my dear, you will start a craze for adorning dancing slippers with decorative brooches!"

Belle's palm pressed against her heart, an involuntary gesture of gratitude for the king's attempt to smooth over her embarrassment.

Audley Seagrave took her hand, then, leading her—pulling her, rather—back toward the Lord Chamberlain's box.

"Well, at least no one will forget my first dance at court,"

Belle offered with a shaky laugh.

But her partner did not accept her invitation to lighten the moment. "You best not shame me so after we are wed," he whispered as he offered a tight smile to the next couple waiting to take to the floor. "Or you'll spend the rest of your days at Culmaily, mired with the unfashionable and ill-bred."

An unforgiving temperament, as well as a jealous one. Quick to blame, and quick to punish. A cold-hearted man, this Aubrey Seagrave, one without the least trace of humor.

So different from the rich vein of mirth that characterized Captain Rye.

Where was her rescuer? Belle paused by the railing, trying to spy him amongst the milling crowds.

"Come along, now, madam, let me return you to your guardians before you make an even greater spectacle of yourself," Seagrave said as he grasped her arm and gave a sharp tug.

But something mulish and contrary had her pulling free of his overbearing touch. "I understand a husband has the right to expect obedience from his wife, sir," she bit out, smoothing down the lace that hung from the end of her sleeve. "But recall, we are not married yet."

He blinked, seemingly taken aback by the sharpness of her tone. "Are not modesty and obedience the chief ornaments of any woman, married or not? But I assure you, you need not worry; I well know how to be master without letting a wife feel the weight of it."

Did he indeed? Perhaps, if his wife had all the intelligence of a widgeon…

"Fie, Audley! Is that any way to speak to a lady?" a voice from just behind her drawled before she could offer her own rebuke.

A warm, lively, *familiar* voice. Accompanied by an easy smile as welcome as the cold of snow in the time of harvest.

Her smile gradually faded, though, as she looked back and

forth between Seagrave and Rye, the tension between humming tight as a taunt bowstring. Were the two men friends? Or, good heavens, perhaps even relations?

"A husband has every right to rebuke an erring wife," Seagrave asserted, his brown eyes narrowing. "Nay, not only the right, but the duty. An imperious wife is a plague to her relatives, a derision to strangers, and a torment not only to her husband, but to herself."

"Wife? I fear you are precipitate in anticipating the lady's favor." Captain Rye offered her an elegant bow, then took her gloved hand in his. "Lady Culmaily has a wealth of other suitors besides yourself."

He pressed a gallant kiss to the top of her hand, then slipped a warm piece of metal into her palm.

Her mother's brooch?

Warm tendrils of relief unfurled in her chest as her eyes shot to his. But Rye was staring not at her, but at her dancing partner.

"Do you presume to number yourself among that group?" Seagrave gave Rye a dismissive sniff. "As if a baroness with expectations of rising even higher would stoop to the level of a younger son. Arrogant as always, I see, brother."

Brother?

"You and Captain Rye are related?" Oh, good heavens. Had she actually squealed?

Surprise and curiosity rippled through the other couples awaiting their turn to dance.

The captain must have felt it, too, for he placed a hand on her arm and drew her toward the back staircase, away from prying eyes.

Seagrave stalked behind them, disgruntlement in every line of his person. "Brothers? Yes, to my shame, and the shame of all our family. A willful, undutiful boy, Zachariah has always been, from the very moment of his birth."

The contempt in the gentleman's voice would have curdled

cream. But Rye only responded with a dry chuckle, a chuckle that said his brother's slight did not matter in the least. A chuckle that urged her to shrug it off without a care, too, just as easily as had he.

But even after only the few brief moments she'd spent in his company this day, Belle could see that chuckle for the lie it clearly was. That tightness about his full lips, the color that leached from his face—his brother's cruel, dismissive words hurt.

"But why did Patty introduce you as Captain Rye?" she asked.

Rye chuckled. "A nickname bestowed upon me by the regiment. Far easier to shout one syllable amid a heated battle than the tediously long-winded 'Zachariah.'"

Zachariah—*Rye*—Seagrave. Better known by his friends as Captain Rye.

"The name suits you, far better than the stiff, biblical Zachariah."

His brother offered another contemptuous sniff. "Rye, a grain used to make intoxicating spirits! A sobriquet far more suited to his character than Zachariah, which means 'God remembers.' I cannot but believe our Heavenly Father would far prefer to forget such a reprobate as he."

"Reprobate?" Belle found herself stepping between the two men, almost as if she wished her person to serve as protection for the younger brother against his elder. "A soldier whom the king himself has praised for his loyalty and courage?"

Audley Seagrave shot a contemptuous glance not at his brother's face, but at his dress uniform. "An unaccountable humor in womankind, being smitten by the showy and superficial. You consider only the drapery of the species, and never cast a thought on the ornaments of the mind that make a man truly of worth. But you would do well to consider, my lady, whether a man who cares more for glittering gee-gaws than for his duty to his family is worthy of your admiration."

"You speak as if familial duty requires me to participate in all of grandfather's foolish political and social machinations!" Rye exclaimed. "Why he believes persuading the king to bestow the Audley earldom on him will expunge the shame of his father's being attainted, I'll never understand."

"And why you have not the least concern for Seagrave honor, I'll never fathom," his brother snapped. "Unless you've been plying your charms on the daughter of the Earl of Audley in hopes of strengthening the family's claim to her father's title?"

"I did not know she was the earl's daughter, not until she told me this afternoon. Besides, unlike you, I don't leap to do Grandfather's bidding whenever he wags a bone in my face."

The elder brother flushed. "There is no shame in showing proper deference to the head of one's house."

"Even when showing such deference means abandoning the girl you've loved since you were a boy?" Rye asked, his voice softening. "Does poor Jenny know what you are about, Lee?"

Belle's fingers tightened around the brooch in her hand. Audley Seagrave already loved another? No wonder his bearing had been so stiff, his manner to her so cold.

She should have been appalled, hearing his affections were already engaged. But the pinch of his lips, the sudden slump of his shoulders at his brother's words—no, she couldn't be angry with him, not truly.

Folly, though, to feel a flutter of guilt, as if somehow she were responsible for interfering with the course of true love. Especially when the pain in his eyes changed to anger, as if he'd only now realized how damning Rye's words must have sounded to her.

"Lady Culmaily," he exclaimed. "My brother knows not of what he speaks. I vow that when we are married, I will give you no call for reproach. I know my duty, even if my brother does not."

"Duty does not ensure affection, or even compatibility. Or appreciation for a wife's intelligence, or spirit," Rye said, the seriousness of his tone drawing her eyes to his. "And duty certainly will not warm your bed at night."

Belle gasped, all the blood rushing to her ears. Had he truly said such an outrageous thing, right here, in the midst of the king's birthday ball?

And had his assertion made her draw closer, rather than back away in offense?

"Cease your folly, Zachariah," Audley Seagrave said, placing a proprietary hand on her arm. "Lady Culmaily is far too much of a lady to be swayed by your dubious charms. She must see how you ply them on her only out of spite, in some ill-fated attempt to thwart grandfather's plans, and my own."

"I assure you, brother, my attentions to the lady have nothing at all to do with you."

The ardency of that low, vibrant voice; the glow of those lush green eyes; the fixed attention, which made her feel as if she were the only lady in the entire room, in the entire world—

Belle's fingers tightened around her mother's brooch, resisting the urge to reach out and trace his furrowed brow, his stern, frowning lips.

"Do you like strawberries, sir?" she heard herself ask Audley Seagrave in a voice she barely recognized.

"Strawberries?" The gentleman blinked, then shuddered. "I hope you are not fond of them, ma'am, for I cannot abide them. A mere taste of that blasted fruit makes me break out in a rash."

Unkind, it was, to make sport of another's misfortune. But one look at the glint of amusement in Rye's eye, the mirth in that one raised eyebrow, and she burbled over with the most unladylike guffaw.

By teaching, if not always by temperament, Arabella Audley knew the most reliable and socially acceptable method was usually the best if she wished to accomplish her goals. Dress as society dictated. Comport herself as society demanded. Follow the advice of those whom she respected.

Marry the man most likely to bring her the Audley title.

But mayhap it was time to take a page out of unconventional Zachariah Seagrave's book and consider other ways of getting what she wanted…

"A pity, sir." Belle gave the captain's brother her deepest curtsey, then slipped her hand inside her gown's pocket slit and set her mother's runaway brooch safely inside a hoop. "Then I fear I must bid you good evening."

"What? Where are you going?"

Belle made him no answer. Taking Rye's—Zachariah's—hand in hers, she tugged, pulling him to the edge of the ballroom, past their fellow dancers, the courtiers and royal retainers, and their fellow attendees. Past his clearly amused grandfather, who raised his eyebrows and tipped his head toward her furiously whispering guardians, then gave her a significant wink.

Belle grinned back, silently accepting his offer to distract her Quarrelsome Custodians while she set a proposition before his grandson.

"Baroness! You can't—you shouldn't! To snatch up a gentleman and walk off with him without even a by-your-leave! Oh, it is most improper…"

Belle smothered a laugh as she pulled Rye past a wide-eyed Page of the Backstairs. Such a comically exaggerated repetition of her own earlier words! She only imagined the acclaim they might win if he and Astley were to add a touch of such humor to their equestrian performances…

"Will you come with me, Captain?" Belle asked, though she slowed her pace not a jot. "I have something of import to discuss with you."

"But where are you taking me? A gentleman must be wary of besmirching his good name," he teased, even as he continued to follow her down the staircase.

"Somewhere we may speak in private," she said, making sure to keep her amusement from seeping into her tone. She may have decided to take a risk on her future, but she needn't allow sentiment to make her completely buffle-headed.

He paused, though, at the bottom of the staircase, setting his back to the rush of servants bustling about them.

"My brother may deem me a Jack among the maids, my lady, but even I have a care for the reputation of a baroness," he said, his tone suddenly serious. "One may, perhaps, steal away from an inattentive crowd in Southwark, but withdrawing from the midst of a royal birthday ball will certainly catch the attention of the *ton*'s gossips."

"It will be of no matter, not if you assent to my proposal."

"And may one inquire, my lady, as to the nature of said proposal?"

Belle humphed. As if he hadn't the least idea!

She did not deign to answer, too busy scouring the passageway for a place where they might talk unobserved. Not that antechamber, not the cloakroom, certainly not in the garderobe—

A servant shouldering open a small door at passageway's end caught her eye. There must be a quieter spot outside…

Following in the servant's steps, she caught the door before it could completely close behind him. Rye allowed her to drag him through it without protest into a large courtyard reeking of the scent of wood smoke. The kitchens must be nearby.

But even more servants were bustling about the yard than in the passageway inside, carrying plates and platters between the palace and a smaller building nearby.

Where, where, where? St. James' Park, perhaps? It lay right behind the palace, did it not? Her guardians had insisted they promenade its tree-lined cockle-shell paths as soon as they'd arrived in town, to see and be seen by fashionable society. Surely at such a late hour the Mall would be empty.

She drew him through the courtyard, past a smaller building that appeared to house the kitchen block, and then around the edge of the palace wall. The sun had set, but a waxing gibbous moon hung high in the cloudless night sky, granting her a sight of the trees of the Park. She caught back a groan as she realized its Mall lay not only further from the palace than she'd remembered, but behind a tall brick wall that lay between park and palace. With no door betwixt the two anywhere in sight. No, the Park would not do.

But, there, just to the back of the palace itself—a smaller, private stretch of lawn…

Rye laughed as she pulled him towards what must be the palace's privy gardens. "What a merry romp you lead me on, madam."

She finally came to a stop beside a low flowerbed filled with dwarf fruit trees and vining roses, far from the noise of the busy courtyard. She stepped closer to her companion, close enough that she could reach out and stroke a finger down the row of silver buttons set on the facings of his uniform if she wished. Not that she would ever act in such a manner!

She tucked her hands neatly against the stomacher of her gown, pressing back against the suddenly wild beating of her heart.

"Captain Seagrave," she began, but then stumbled to a stop. Where had the calm, collected tone her father had always counseled her a successful negotiator should employ gone? Good heavens, her voice had nearly *squeaked*!

"Lady Culmaily," he answered, lowering his voice as the

music from the ballroom above came to a halt.

Gathering both breath and courage, she forced her eyes to his. "You are as yet unmarried, Captain?"

Light from the palace windows above set shadows dancing over his face, making it difficult for her to discern his expression. But she could certainly hear his low chuckle.

"Yes, my lady," he answered, his tone as falsely docile as that of a boy answering to a schoolmaster.

"And unlike your elder brother, not tied by inclination or prior claim to another?"

"No, my lady."

"And do you have any intention of—any desire to—to one day…" Oh, why should the word be so hard to force between her lips?

"To wed?" she finally managed to blurt.

He tilted his head, his face abruptly moving from shadow to light. She saw that provoking eyebrow lifting, his gloved hand rising, too. A single finger began to tap a slow, infuriating beat against his chin.

"Have I? I don't know as I've ever considered the matter overmuch," he finally offered, his tone exaggeratedly nonchalant.

Belle caught back a laugh. Why should she be so amused by behavior that in any other man would have annoyed? Perhaps because she had never met a man who flung about his charm with all the ease of a cloak tossed carelessly about his shoulders?

"And if you *were* to consider it?" she asked, feigning equal nonchalance as she stepped closer to the flower bed and drew a finger down a thickly haired stem of a rose. Rich, voluptuous, the scent of the blossom rising from it, with just a hint of honey and raspberry—not strawberry—tickling her senses.

"Hmmm." His eyes raised to the dark, starlit sky above, he nodded, then shook his head, then nodded again, and then a third time. As if he were posing the pros and cons to himself in that very moment, acknowledging or disagreeing with his own internal assessments by turn.

"Some day, perhaps," he finally offered, leaning back against the low wall of a flower bed, gazing down at his boots as if they were discussing nothing of more importance than how well his valet had managed to make them shine. "If a suitable lady were to one day cross my path."

A surprisingly sharp sting, the intimation that he hadn't met such a lady yet. A sting not just to her pride, but, far more surprisingly, to her heart. Almost as if she wished to make a match of affection, rather than an alliance to secure her father's title.

"And what sort of lady would suit?" she asked, frowning away the wayward feeling. "One who could offer land and capital enough to establish the best stud farm in all of England, perhaps?"

His abrupt shift away from the wall told her that her guess had hit home. She turned back to the vining rose to hide a satisfied smile. Though Zachariah Seagrave clearly enjoyed performing with the Astleys, a man of such intelligence and ambition surely must want something more. Something upon which he might put his own stamp, something he would be the one to manage and control.

"Cruel, my lady, to dangle a dream in front of a gentleman when he has little chance of realizing it."

"Little chance? Surely many a lady currently in search of an eligible *parti* could offer the like."

Belle's hand clenched around her mother's brooch. Why had she mentioned other ladies? A tactical mistake, to remind him he had other options.

Time to stop feinting, and go directly on attack. To take her place among her Audley ancestresses by acting as audaciously as they had.

"But only I could also offer him—offer *you*—a title, as well as a place to train and breed all the horses you like. All you'd need do is promise to leave the direction of the estate, of Audley Priory, to me." Belle turned away from the vining rose and gazed directly into his eyes. "Zachariah Seagrave, will you marry me?"

Her stomach clenched as he looked down at her. Not with the expression of eagerness and anticipation she'd expected, but with a frown of—of disappointment? Had she been entirely mistaken in the mutuality of their regard?

"I think you forget, Lady Culmaily, a peeress in her own right cannot confer her title upon her spouse. A commoner will ever remain a commoner, no matter who he marries."

Was that all? But she could easily reassure him on that head.

Belle stepped closer, close enough for the musk of the pomade keeping his unruly curls in line to tickle her nose. "But my guardians, and your grandfather, together can make the case to the king, and Parliament's Committee on Privileges, that our union would be the neatest solution to a dispute over another, higher title."

"You also forget, ma'am, in what disdain my grandfather holds me. He'd hardly agree to cede me the title, not when he has my perfect brother to hand."

Belle heard the anger in Rye's voice, but underneath it, pain, too, and a surprisingly wistful longing, a longing for a family he believed had cast him aside.

A family, perhaps, she could help him regain, even if she could never regain her own…

"He finds you frustrating, perhaps, but he doesn't hold you in contempt," she said. "I even think a part of him admires you for not bowing to his dictates."

"What? Why would you think such a thing?"

"Because when he spoke of his brashly disobedient younger grandson, I heard not only chagrin, but a deep well of affection in his voice. If you wished to reconcile with your family, our marriage would be a welcome first step, would it not?"

"And what then? I bow and scrape to any gentleman

grandfather thinks important, no matter my own views of the fellow? I embrace his care for rank and privilege above all, as you do?"

"Is that what you think?" she exclaimed. "That I value rank and privilege above all?"

"Do you not?" His gaze turned up to the ballroom window. "Most here tonight do."

"But I am not like—I thought you had seen—"

"No?" He spun about, then stepped close, until barely a whisper of space remained between them. "Then tell me. Tell me why you are so determined your father's title not pass from your hands. So damned determined you actually contemplated marrying my brother, a man whose heart will never belong to you."

Belle stepped back, blinking. For years, the quest to regain her father's title had haunted her every waking moment. Every member of her Contentious Cabinet spoke of little else. The importance of lineage, of tradition, of family honor. The duty to maintain noble bloodlines. The necessity of keeping a proper distance between the aristocracy and upstart gentry such as Henry de Audley and the elder Audley Seagrave.

But no such orthodox arguments would sway a man as unconstrained by convention as Captain Rye.

The bite of his words, though, had reminded her of her own reason. Not those of her father, or her guardians, or the leaders of the *ton*. The one dismissed as little more than sentimental twaddle by everyone to whom she had dared to confide it. The one she had long ago buried deep in her heart.

If she wanted him to agree to her plan, she knew she would have to share it with him.

"My father—he taught me—all those of noble title, we have a duty, a duty to the land, a duty to those who earn their livelihoods from it," she began, her voice tripping and stumbling to articulate something she'd spent so much effort repressing.

"How can I ensure our people will be properly taken care of if Audley Priory is given to another?"

"A concern, indeed, if Henry de Audley were to inherit, rather than my grandfather," he acknowledged. "One would have to search far beyond London to discover a more self-indulgent, or spendthrift, macaroni than that gentleman. But I believe my grandfather has a stronger claim than de Audley. And if he, and through him, my brother, were to be entrusted with your father's estate, you would have little cause to worry."

"But they wouldn't know the land, know its people! Not the way I do!"

"Perhaps not, at least not straight away. But no matter how little they esteem me, it would be a falsehood for me to claim my grandfather and brother are not men of duty, and of honor. I promise you, both will take proper care of Audley Priory's tenants, and its poor."

"But that is not enough. Not for me!" Belle cried, her voice raw with pain. "I want, no, I *need*, to have a say in the running of the estate. Who else would know whether or not to renew a tenant's lease? Know which farming innovations would best serve the Priory's land and people, and which would not be worth the trouble of disrupting the old ways to implement? Who would care to tend the vault and the churchyard where my ancestors lie? My grandparents, my aunts and uncles, my father and mother? And my dear, dear brother, too?"

Belle shuddered, shocked by what her words revealed. She'd long pushed grief to the side, burying it deep within her, a fruitless distraction from her more tangible goals. Why, then, should all that anguish, all that loss, somehow come hurtling back to the surface whenever she found herself in the vicinity of Zachariah Seagrave?

Would he think her weak? Foolish, to fear abandoning a family who had long left her?

She turned her back to him, staring out over the lawn,

struggling to regain the composure that had abandoned her, too.

The hand he laid with such gentleness, such care, on her shoulder—too much, too much—

She jerked free of his touch, her hand reaching inside her skirt to clench about her mother's brooch. Time to stop wallowing in mere feelings and return to the actual issue at hand.

"Could you promise me that your brother, who believes modesty and obedience the chief ornaments of any woman, would allow me to direct the running of the estate as I saw fit?" she asked.

"Hardly," he admitted. "But do you think any other man would?"

"I'm not asking any other man. I'm asking *you*, Zachariah Seagrave." Belle took his gloved hand in hers. Squeezing his strong fingers tight, as if she could squeeze all of her intentions, her need, her leap of faith, directly from her hands to his. "Because you challenge me. Think me capable. And admire in me what other men scorn."

"I do, Baroness," he said, his voice suddenly, unexpectedly grave. He squeezed her hand in return. "You are like no other lady I've ever known."

Belle's breath caught. How could a heart pounding so heavy, so hard, soar as high as the moon?

And then crash so shudderingly to the ground, when his hand slipped from hers, fisted at his sides.

"But do you think *me* capable?" he challenged. "Admire in *me* what other men scorn? Or am I only the most expeditious means to your desired end?"

Belle blinked, taken aback by the sudden vehemence of his tone.

"My lady, I've spent my entire life resisting my family's attempts to control me, to constrain me. When I was a boy, I refused to bow and scrape to schoolmates just because of their high rank, as my brother insisted I must. And when my grandfather first introduced me to society, I refused to kowtow to the men whom my grandfather insisted were important, for no other reason than the title they held, or the sway they had at court. I even joined the army, rather than take holy orders as my grandfather demanded, just to escape their unending pressure to conform. So you see, I will never allow myself to be relegated to the role of useful pawn, pushed across the chessboard at another's will."

Belle felt her temper flair. "You, a pawn? As if a lady's life is anything but! Especially a lady under the guardianship of five gentlemen! Continually constrained and controlled and shuffled between them, to be used as each sees fit."

"But I—"

"At least you were allowed to attend school. My guardians yanked me from Patty and all my friends at the Abbey School without even a by-your-leave."

"I had not considered—"

"Could I leave my guardians and make my own way in the world? Join the army? Put myself on public display as a performer in an equestrian show? Could I do anything to regain my father's title *but* choose the lesser of two marital evils?"

"Yes!" he exclaimed as he grasped her shoulders. "You could, and have. You proposed to me, remember? Not to de Audley, or to Lee, or even to my grandfather. To *me*."

"But you have not accepted!" she cried.

"No. Because you offered only so you might become master of the chessboard at my expense. I tell you again, I won't be your pawn. Not for a stud farm. Not for a title. Not even for the chance to wed a woman who takes my very breath away."

Belle's own breath caught at the vehemence of Rye's words. Could he truly harbor such strong feelings for her?

Feelings that, she suddenly, terrifyingly realized, might just match her own for him?

"Then make me a counterproposal," she heard herself whisper.

"A counterproposal?"

"Yes. You say you won't marry if it means becoming a pawn. What do you wish marriage to be instead?"

"More than simply your proposed contract for wealth and power," he said, throwing up his hands. "And certainly more than one party taking control of the other, whether that party be the more typical gentleman, or, under your proposal, the less typical lady."

Belle bit her lip. "A… a love match, do you mean?"

"Yes," Rye confirmed. "I've been told my parents wed for love. But they perished long before I was old enough to pay much attention to the workings of their marriage."

"As did mine," Belle said. "Marry for love, I mean. But from what I remember of them, my father certainly exercised all authority. Is that not what you wish?"

"No! I have a far different example in mind. The example of Philip and Patty, which I have before my eyes every single day."

Belle's entire body stilled as visions of Patty and her Mr. Astley, working together, riding together, laughing together, flashed across her mind. Even after only a few brief moments in their company at court, and later, watching their joint efforts during the riding exhibition, Belle could tell that their relationship had taken root in far different ground than she'd ever dreamed would be possible for any marriage she might contract.

Hands clenching, she took a halting step towards to Rye.

"Not a submission of one to the other, but a friendship? A companionship? Is that what you envision?"

"Yes, but not only that. I want a marriage in which both husband and wife *talk* to each other, *listen* to each other. Not one in which they just demand every expectation society, or they themselves, hold must be fulfilled with no regard to the preferences, or happiness, of the other. Not as my family has always treated me."

"And not as my guardians have acted towards me," Belle replied. "You wish a marriage in which each makes time to talk with the other, to ask questions of the other? To discover the other's wants and needs?"

"Yes, and even more. A marriage based on the sharing of joys and burdens, one leavened with caring, and perhaps, eventually, even love. Having borne daily witness to such a marriage these past three years, I cannot bring myself to settle for less."

Belle's ribs, already constrained by her corset, pulled even tighter, making it difficult to catch her breath. He wouldn't marry her. For he didn't, *couldn't,* care for her like that. Not so soon...

"Then I must leave my father and mother," she whispered, hanging her head. "And my brother. Leave them in the vault at Audley Priory, leave them, leave him, to the care of strangers who know nothing, remember nothing, of them."

But then she felt hands, ungloved hands, squeezing her shoulders. *His* hands. A strange yet welcome shudder of awareness shivered down her spine.

"Love for your family is what truly drives you, Lady Culmaily? An unfamiliar feeling for one such as me, who has too often allowed anger at his relations to be his spur. But not one beyond my comprehension. Certainly one worth honoring."

Belle blinked as tears, unexpected, embarrassing, pricked at the corners of her eyes. How could this man see her so clearly, when she could barely see herself?

He gave her shoulders another light squeeze, then turned her to face him. "If I thought I might have a chance, even a small one, of gaining a place in the circle of such a love—of sharing in your pleasures and joys, as well as your pains and sorrows, of debating decisions about *our* estate *together*, rather than each off in his own corner, occupied only with his own concerns—well, that would be an opportunity far more tempting than any stud farm you could offer. Far more tempting even than your father's earldom."

His warm hands cupped her face, drew her close. "An opportunity a man would be a fool not to grasp."

"Do you claim to hold me in such high regard?" she asked, the quiver in her voice matching the one in her insides. "Even after knowing me for less than a day?"

"'Where both deliberate, / the love is slight, / Who ever loved, that loved not at first sight?'" he quoted. "I believe the only love in question here, then, is yours. Could you ever come to love *me*, Arabella Audley?"

Love? Dare to love Rye?

Could she?

Belle pulled off her gloves and tucked them inside her hoop pocket, next to her mother's brooch. She pressed a hand against the silver buttons of his coat, and then, more daringly, a bare finger against the sweep of his mouth. "I believe I could, Zachariah Seagrave. Why else would I feel as if I am both about to fly over the edge of the cliffs of Dover and sail right up to the stars whenever you are near? Now come here, as I do not wish to regret never experiencing the taste of strawberries on my future husband's lips."

At her whispered words, those lips quirked beneath her finger, then fanned into a wide, warm grin. A flash of unfamiliar sensation darted down her finger, her hand, her entire body, as if she'd been shot through with electric fire. But it did not repulse, that fire; it drew her towards him, her north pole snapping in place to his south.

"Then allow me to give you a foretaste of a pleasure I promise we will often share once we are wed," he whispered, his arms slipping about her waist and drawing her near.

He tasted not of the promised strawberries, but of salt, and heat, and the orange-butter of her own lip salve. For an instant,

Belle thought to tease him for it, until his tongue traced the seam of her lips and set all rational thought to flight.

Those lips parted, astonishingly eager to dart and delve in turn. But the touch of her tongue to his turned her shockingly feral, suddenly wild with the need to draw his body, his mind, his very soul, into hers. Shivering with want, she rose on her toes, threw her arms about his neck, and drew his head down…

And found her eagerness matched by the hunger of his own. She nearly cried out when he pressed her body to his, but his mouth stoppered hers, his lips, his tongue plunging and plundering like the cavalry officer he'd once been, and she a castle under his siege.

But he was not the only one who could wage war. Belle met him thrust for thrust, parry for parry, besieging his body, too, until they both panted with want.

Belle did not know how long they'd battled until he finally pulled free of her mouth and raised his head from hers.

"Tell me I'm more to you than only a means to an end," he demanded, his expression fierce, yet vulnerable, in the suddenly bright moonlight. "Tell me you want me for myself, as least as much as you want me for what our alliance might allow you to regain."

"More," she whispered, hoping her face, her voice, would convey the truth of her heart. "Oh, so very, very much more—"

He cut off her words with another kiss, fierce, triumphant, as if by devouring her declaration, he might make it his. Make her his.

They kissed for hours, eons, the shadows of the couples twirling in the ballroom above them dancing across the gardens around them. Belle heard music, then a low, distant hissing buzzing in her ears. The sound of her own blood singing through her veins, singing of life, of want, of possibilities she'd never before imagined?

A rapid succession of sharp reports, followed by a deafening roar of thunder, suddenly smothered all sound. Her eyes, which had drifted shut sometime during Rye's impassioned kisses, jerked wide, her head turning toward the heavens. Were they about to be deluged?

She looked up but could spy not even a single cloud in the clear, moonlit sky.

"Illuminations!" Rye exclaimed, pulling her back against his chest, then pointing toward the opposite end of the park. "In honor of the King's birthday."

She jerked as a flash brighter than the most brilliant lightning shot across the sky.

He pulled her tight into the shelter of his arms, allowing her to watch the display from the safety of his embrace. Oh, she'd heard the noise made by crackers and squibs thrown by boys in the street before, but those sounds were nothing to these! And the sight! Roman candles spraying across the sky like fountains, rockets of fire spiraling like corkscrews, heavy globes spitting, then exploding, like seeds blown from a dandelion clock—if the blower could summon the force of all four wind gods simultaneously.

"Have you never seen a pyrotechnic display, Lady Culmaily?" Rye asked.

"No," she answered, turning to rub her cheek against his.

"I dare say, then, it would be difficult for the baroness to distinguish between the meteors of delight inflaming the sky and those inflaming her heart," an amused voice from behind them declared.

The king?

Belle jerked from Rye's arms and sank into a deep curtsey. When she rose, she saw King George on the path before her, a knowing smile quirking across his broad face. Several of his courtiers stood to his one side, Patty Astley and her husband to his other. And behind them, Glenlyon, Mowbray, and the rest of Belle's guardians and their wives.

Aunt Elizabeth offered her a gentle smile, and Patty laced her arm through her husband's and grinned.

"Your highness," Belle whispered, her hand clutching at Rye's sleeve and holding on tight. "Forgive us for intruding on your grounds and your privacy. But we—"

"'But we' indeed," the king said with a chuckle. "It would seem that fate has forged a solution to the vexing problem of the Audley earldom. Send your grandfather to speak to Bute tomorrow, Captain. If he is willing to drop his suit in your favor, we will convey our royal recommendation to the Committee on Privileges that the title be declared extinct, then granted to you. After, of course, you and Lady Culmaily marry."

Another burst of light illuminating the sky interrupted Rye's bow of assent, showering sparks of white, red, and blue over the treetops.

"But enough of that!" the king declared with a careless wave. "What man would wish to talk of business with such dazzling illuminations to hand? Quiet, now, and watch!"

The collected observers gasped and exclaimed as blue stars and white shot across the sky. But Belle only had eyes for her captain as she reached inside her pocket hoop and retrieved her mother's brooch.

With careful fingers, she pinned it to the lapel of his coat.

His sudden intake of breath, the movement of his hand, told her he understood the significance of her action.

The tip of his finger played across the points of the flared crown at the top of the brooch, then dipped lower, tracing the heart shape at its center. Then he pressed that fingertip against her lips, whispering his acceptance of her wordless promise.

"Before my eye, my dearest, darling Arabella, I pledge: no star to thee..."

THE END

THANK YOU

Thanks for reading *Not Quite a Countess*. I hope it gave you as much pleasure in the reading as it gave me in the writing.

Would you consider writing a review? Reader reviews on Goodreads, LibraryThing, and other social networking and book retailer sites are especially valuable for e-books. I'm grateful for all reviews, critical or admiring, and if you take the time to write one of *NQaC*, you have my thanks.

If you'd like to know when my next book becomes available, follow my Amazon author page.

To find out about discounts, giveaways, and other Bliss Bennet-related info, sign up for her newsletter (on her website, www.blissbennet.com), follow her on BlueSkySocial (@BlissBennet.bsky.social), or like her Author Facebook (blissbennetauthor) or Instagram page (blissbennetwrites).

AUTHOR'S NOTE

In the prologue of each book in the *Audacious Ladies of Audley* series, five female cousins participate in a family ritual honoring their audacious ancestresses, a ritual meant to inspire them to make their own audacious choices in life and love. I thought about writing a short story or novella prequel featuring one of those early ancestors, but was concerned that readers of my Regency stories might not want to take up a story set in a far earlier time period. But perhaps they might welcome a Georgian-set romance?

And so the idea of casting the girls' grandmother as the lead of an Audacious Audley prequel popped into my head. A prequel set during the early years of the reign of George III, telling the story of how the lady who became the cousins' Grandmother Audley found and married her earl.

After I began to brainstorm possible plot lines for such a story, however, I soon realized I had written myself into a corner. Because although Grandmother Audley's granddaughters were Audleys by birth, Grandmother, who is called the "Countess of Audley" in her brief appearance in the Prologue of *Not Quite a Scandal*, could only be an Audley by *marriage*. Would she even regard herself as one of the "audacious ladies of Audley" if she had only married into the family?

I could think of only one way around the bind I had created: if the Audley title was allowed to pass not only through the male, but also through the female, line, then Grandmother Audley might be both an Audley by birth *and* by marriage.

But was this historically possible? Did any actual woman inherit an English peerage in her own right during the eighteenth century?

As most Regency readers know, the majority of British peerages were created for men, and could be passed down only to their male descendants. But a deep dive into the minutiae of British inheritance law taught me that a few titles in the past had been created with "special remainders," or, as the *Oxford English Dictionary* defines it, "the right of succession to a peerage expressly assigned to a certain person or line of descent in default of male issue in the direct line." In other words, if a peer died without a son or other direct male descendant, the special remainder would kick in, allowing the title to pass to someone else specified by the terms of the remainder.

On very rare occasions, that "someone else" was a woman.

OK. So Grandmother Audley *could possibly* have been an Audley by birth if she inherited the Audley title directly, rather than only marrying into the peerage.

Next, I had to find out if any historical women *had* inherited a peerage during the time I imagined my story would be set.

Back to the library…

Where I discovered the fascinating case of Elizabeth Sutherland, who inherited the title Countess of Sutherland in 1771 through her father after a protracted court battle.

Elizabeth's parents both died of a putrid fever in 1766, shortly after her first birthday. Elizabeth's father was the the 18th Earl of Sutherland, and Elizabeth was his only surviving child. Because the Sutherland earldom, a Scottish title, had once been inherited by a woman (in the early sixteenth century), Elizabeth's guardians argued that *she* should now be granted the title Countess of Sutherland.

But several of Elizabeth's relatives disagreed. Her father's distant cousin, Sir Robert Gordon, 4th baronet, and an even more distant relation, George Sutherland of Force, the 14th Laird of Force, each made counter-claims, arguing that *he* should be named the next Sutherland earl.

For years, each of the three claimants (or, in Elizabeth's case, her five guardians), petitioned the king, submitted evidence to Parliament's Committee on Privileges, and published accounts explaining why he (or she) was the rightful heir to the earldom. After six years of debate, and seven long days of official hearings at the bar of the House of Peers, the Committee on Privileges at long last issued its decision:

> *Resolved and Adjudged, by the Lords Spiritual and Temporal, in Parliament assembled, That the Claimant, Elizabeth Sutherland, has a Right to the Title, Honour, and Dignity, of the Earldom of Sutherland, as Heir of the Body of William who was Earl of Sutherland in 1275.*

As you can tell from reading *Not Quite A Countess*, I've drawn heavily on young Elizabeth Sutherland's history in crafting Arabella Audley's quest to win back her father's English earldom.

Belle is not the only audacious lady in *Not Quite a Countess* whom I modeled after a real-life woman. The name "Astley" might ring a bell with historical romance readers; Astley's Amphitheater, an actual London performance venue of the period, is mentioned in many a Regency romance, as well as in the works of Jane Austen and Charles Dickens. But few are likely familiar with the name Philip Astley, the man often credited as the father of the modern circus. Even fewer have likely heard of his wife, Patty, who has largely disappeared from the historical record. Steve Ward's informative book, *Father of the Modern*

Circus 'Billy Buttons': The Life & Times of Philip Astley (Pen &
Sword, 2018) provided a wealth of information about Astley, a
former cavalry officer who became the most lauded equestrian
performer in Europe during the late eighteenth and early
nineteenth centuries. Vanessa Toulmin's excellent article, "'My
wife to conclude performs the rest'—Patty Astley, the First Lady
of the Circus" (which reprints in its entirety the 1773 pamphlet,
*A Short Description of the Various Feats of Activity Exhibited at
Astley's British Riding School*) served as a great aid in fleshing out
Patty's role as Belle's old schoolmate.

To learn more about other sources I drew upon in the crafting of
Not Quite a Countess (including such topics as fireworks,
macaroni men, and what to do if you lose a slipper while
dancing at the King's Birthday Ball), check out my website,
www.blissbennet.com.

ACKNOWLEDGEMENTS

No novel is ever completed without the help, encouragement, and good will of many people besides its author. My deepest gratitude to:

My romance writing friends and colleagues, in particular my fellow authors in the New England Romance Writers and Regency Fiction Writers communities. I appreciate all the knowledge and expertise members of each group share with generosity and good humor.

Critique and accountability partners, who continue to praise, suggest, and criticize in just the right balance: Janet Campbell, Gail Eastwood, Jessica Gibbons, Wendy LaCapra, AG Meiers, Gayle Parness, and Tricia Woods. I continue to grow and learn as a writer from each of you.

My publishing support team, especially Elena K of L1graphics, who continues to create the book covers of my dreams. Thank you so much!

England-based researcher extraordinaire Andrew Lewis, who made a special trip to the British Library for me to dig up first-hand sources on the Elizabeth Sutherland inheritance case.

My toddler dinner neighbors, especially now that our toddlers have all flown the nest. Thanks to Jessica, Trey, Anita, Norbert, Anne Marie, and Roger for *still* listening to all my talk about Romancelandia, self-publishing, and sex. And special thanks to Jessica for the lovely author and cover photos.

Mr. Bennet (my own, not Elizabeth's), who continues to support me with funny comics and razor-sharp analytical skills. And my own young Miss Bennet, especially now that she is becoming an intelligent, independent woman (and who agreed to don the elaborate dress I crafted for *NQAC* and not laugh too much during photo shoot for the book's cover). I love you both so much.

And last, but certainly not least, you, my readers and reviewers. Thank you for taking a chance on my books. There are so many romances of all types being written and published today; it is an honor to know that you've chosen to spend your time with mine.

SOMETHING ABOUT BLISS

Award-winning historical romance author Bliss Bennet writes smart, edgy novels for readers who love history as much as they love romance. Despite being born and bred in New England, Bliss has always been fascinated by the history of that country across the pond, particularly the politically-volatile period known as the English Regency. Though she's visited Britain several times, Bliss continues to make her home in New England along with her spouse and an ever-multiplying collection of historical reference books.

Bliss's Regency-set historical romances have been praised as "savvy, sensual, and engrossing" by *USA Today*, "catnip for the Historical Romance reader" by *Bookworlder*, "romantic, funny, touching, and extremely well-researched" by *All About Romance*, and "everything you want in a great historical romance" by *The Reading Wench*.

If you'd like to know when Bliss's next book becomes available, follow her Amazon author page.

To find out about discounts, giveaways, and other Bliss Bennet-related info, sign up for her newsletter, follow her on BlueSkySocial (@BlissBennet.bsky.social), or like her Author Facebook (blissbennetauthor) or Instagram page (blissbennetwrites).

EAGER FOR MORE FROM BLISS?

THE AUDACIOUS LADIES
OF AUDLEY

Delphie and Spencer's story: *Not Quite a Marriage*

Spencer Burnett, Viscount Stiles, once swore he'd left England for good. Yet after five years of self-imposed exile in West Africa, he's no longer the same spoiled, selfish boy who ran away from a domineering father, a disappointed grandmother, and a decidedly unwanted wife. Proving himself to the family he abandoned will be no easy task. But he hardly expects his formerly docile wife will be the hardest to convince. When Philadelphia refuses to accept his apologies—or to allow him back into her bed—Spencer finds himself tempting her into a bargain he cannot afford to lose.

Philadelphia Burnett's desires were once as vast as the sky. But now, after suffering one devastating loss after another, the only thing she allows herself to want is a home. When Delphie's estranged rake of a husband returns from a five-years' absence to claim the estate promised to *her*, Delphie resolves to fight him every step of the way. Beechcombe Park will be a sanctuary for her, and for the wayward Audley cousins she promised her sister she'd always protect. She cannot, will not, suffer even one more loss. Especially not the loss of her heart...

Sheba and Noel's story: *Not Quite a Scandal*

Publishers' *Weekly* **BookLife Prize Semifinalist**

An inheritance lost. A betrothal threatened. A scandal brewing…

Outspoken Bathsheba Honeychurch knows how difficult it is for an unmarried woman, even a Quaker, to successfully champion political change. Her solution? Wed best friend Ash Griffin and begin remaking the world. But the arrival of Ash's worldly cousin with unthinkable news puts Sheba's dreams for the future suddenly at risk…

The death of Noel Griffin's grandfather exposes an appalling betrayal: Noel is *not* the heir to the Silliman earldom, despite what the late earl raised him to believe. Still, the only honorable course is to accept his widowed grandmother's bitter charge: find the true heir, disentangle him from his religious community, and tutor him in the responsibilities and privileges of a title Noel assumed would be his. He certainly won't allow a presumptuous, irritating Quakeress to keep him from his duty —no matter how fascinating he finds her...

When scandal threatens both their reputations, can Sheba and Noel look beyond past dreams and imagine a new world— together?

THE PENNINGTONS

Kit's story: *A Rebel without a Rogue*

A woman striving for justice

Fianna Cameron has devoted her life to avenging the death of her father, hanged as a traitor during the Irish Rebellion of 1798. Now, on the eve of her thirtieth birthday, only one last miscreant remains: Major Christopher Pennington, who both oversaw her father's execution and maligned his honor. Fianna risks everything to travel to London and confront the man who has haunted her every nightmare. Only after her pistol misfires does she realize her sickening mistake: the Pennington she wounded is far too young to be her intended target.

A man who will protect his family at all costs

Rumors of being shot by a spurned mistress might burnish the reputation of a rake, but for Kit Pennington, determined to win a seat in Parliament, such salacious gossip is a nightmare. To regain his good name, Kit vows to track down his mysterious attacker and force her to reveal why she fired on him. Accepting an acquaintance's mistress as an ally in his search is risky enough, but when Kit begins to develop feelings for the icy, ethereal Miss Cameron, more than his political career is in danger.

As their search begins to unearth long-held secrets, Kit and Fianna find themselves caught between duty to family and their beliefs in what's right. How can you balance the competing demands of loyalty and justice—especially when you add love to the mix.

Sibilla's story: *A Man without a Mistress*

A man determined to atone for the past

For seven long years, Sir Peregrine Sayre has tried to assuage his guilt over the horrifying events of his twenty-first birthday by immersing himself in political work—and by avoiding all entanglements with the ladies of the *ton*. But when his mentor sends him on a quest to track down purportedly penitent prostitutes, the events of his less-than-innocent past threaten not only his own political career, but the life of a vexatious viscount's daughter as well.

A woman who will risk anything for the future

Raised to be a political wife, but denied the opportunity by her father's untimely death, Sibilla Pennington has little desire to wed as soon as her period of mourning is over. Why should she have to marry just so her elder brothers might be free of her hoydenish ways and her blazingly angry grief? To delay their plans, Sibilla vows only to accept a betrothal with a man as politically astute as was her father—and, in retaliation for her brothers' amorous peccadillos, only one who has never kept a mistress. Surely there is no such man in all of London.

When Sibilla's attempt to free a reformed maidservant from the clutches of a former procurer throw her into the midst of Per's penitent search, she finds herself inextricably drawn to the cool, reserved baronet. But as the search grows ever more dangerous,

Sibilla's penchant for risk taking cannot help but remind Per of the shames he's spent years trying to outrun. Can Per continue to hide the guilt and ghosts of his past without endangering his chance at a passionate future with Sibilla?

Theo's story: *A Lady without a Lord*

A viscount convinced he's a failure

For years, Theodosius Pennington has tried to forget his myriad shortcomings by indulging in wine, women, and witty bonhomie. But now that he's inherited the title of Viscount Saybrook, it's time to stop ignoring his responsibilities. Finding the perfect husband for his headstrong younger sister seems a good first step. Until, that is, his sister's dowry goes missing . . .

A lady determined to succeed

Harriot Atherton has a secret: it is she, not her steward father, who maintains the Saybrook account books. But Harry's precarious balancing act begins to totter when the irresponsible new viscount unexpectedly returns to Lincolnshire, the painfully awkward boy of her childhood now a charming yet vulnerable man. Unfortunately, Theo is also claiming financial malfeasance. Can her father's wandering wits be responsible for the lost funds? Or is she?

As unlikely attraction flairs between dutiful Harry and playful Theo, each learns there is far more to the other than devoted daughter and happy-go-lucky lord. But if Harry succeeds at protecting her father, discovering the missing money, and keeping all her secrets, will she be in danger of failing at something equally important—finding love?

Benedict's story: *A Sinner without a Saint*

When an honorable artist…

Benedict Pennington's greatest ambition is not to paint a masterpiece, but to make the world's greatest art accessible to all by establishing England's first national art museum. Success in persuading a reluctant philanthropist to donate his collection of Old Master paintings brings his dream tantalizingly close to reality. Until Viscount Dulcie, the object of Benedict's illicit adolescent desire, begins to court the donor's granddaughter, set on winning the paintings for himself . . .

Meets a hedonistic viscount…

Sinclair Milne, Lord Dulcie, far prefers collecting innovative art and dallying with handsome men than burdening himself with a wife. But when rivals imply Dulcie's refusal to pursue wealthy Miss Adler and her paintings is due to lingering tender feelings for Benedict Pennington, Dulcie vows to prove them wrong. Not only will he woo her away from the holier-than-thou painter, he'll also placate his matchmaking father in the process.

Can sinner and saint both win at love?

But when Benedict is dragooned into painting his portrait, Dulcie finds himself once again drawn to the intense artist. Can the sinful viscount entice the wary painter into a casual liaison, one that will put neither their reputations, nor their feelings, at risk? Or will the not-so-saintly artist demand something far more vulnerable—his heart?

TURN THE PAGE FOR A SNEAK PREVIEW OF *NOT QUITE A MARRIAGE,* the next book in *The Audacious Ladies of Audley* series!

FROM NOT QUITE A MARRIAGE

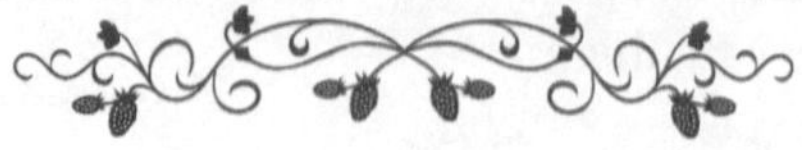

When Spencer Burnett, courtesy titled Baron Stiles, had left England for Sierra Leone at the tender age of three and twenty, more than five long years ago, he'd been utterly certain he'd never return. What in this blasted country could ever tempt him? A grandmother who wept tears of frustration at the very sight of him? A father determined to bend him to his iron will, with no regard for any wish of his own? A sickly wife he barely knew?

A babe, cold and dead in the ground?

But yet here he stood on the side of the dusty Surrey road, once again staring at the hedge of hornbeams lining the drive of his grandmother's beloved Beechcombe Park. If he'd still been the same selfish, callow creature of his youth, he'd be dashing after the post chaise churning up the Guildford to Leatherhead road about now, begging to be let back on, eager to continue to London and partake in all the debaucheries town presumably still had to offer.

Or, at least, eager to torment his father by so partaking.

But Spencer was no longer that same boy, brimming with angry certainties and childish resentments. He'd become a man, one determined to accept his responsibilities and atone for his faults. Ready, at long last, to face his guilt.

He doffed his hat and waved it at Stephen Gabbidon and his daughter, his traveling companions these past two months. Neither had ever left Sierra Leone before, never mind tried to navigate a sprawling metropolis like London. But the letter of introduction he'd given them to his old school friend Noel Griffin would stand them in far better stead than would his own presence in town. Unlike Spencer, Griff had never pissed his good name against the walls in a vain attempt to declare his independence from an overbearing father. With Griff's help, Miss Gabbidon would soon be settled in the school for which she was intended, and her father granted an audience with Earl Bathurst or one of his underlings at the Office of War and the Colonies, where he would present the settlers' petition for greater self-governance in the colony.

Spencer would have to rehabilitate his reputation among men of sense and accomplishment before Bathurst would ever grant him an audience himself. He might have learned to value diplomacy and tact during his years in Africa, but such skills would be useless if he couldn't prove to the Secretary that he was a man worth listening to.

Spencer rubbed his tightly-clenched jaw. Ridiculous, it was, to keep appointing Europeans to public offices in the colony when nearly half of them fell sick and died within a year of emigrating. Almost as ridiculous as the overspending on needlessly lavish public buildings, or the governor's increasingly belligerent attitude towards the Ashantee. Spencer had written to tell the politicians back in England as much, but had received nothing but off-putting, noncommittal replies.

Still, he could hardly blame them. Why should any man of sense give credence to him, when he'd spent so much of his young adulthood deliberately cultivating a reputation as a rebellious, care-for-nothing wastrel?

Repairing his relationships with his family would be the first battle in a far longer campaign to prove his worth to the men in London who moved the levers of political power. Perhaps, at long last, he might even win his father's regard. If the Earl of Morse asked the Colonial Secretary to meet with him, Bathurst would have to listen, rather than simply file away his letters as the ignorant ravings of a self-aggrandizing popinjay.

After setting his hat back on his head, Spencer pulled up the strap of his portmanteau and slung it over his shoulder. Time, now, to take that first step. Not the one from gate to house—Humphrey Repton had designed the grounds of his grandmother's estate, and its short drive was noted throughout the county for its beauty and grace—but the one aimed at making amends to the family he'd left so callously behind. That beloved but disappointed grandmother. His infuriating, never-to-be-pleased father.

And to his cipher of a wife.

As he turned a corner of the drive, he spied the warm red bricks of Beechcombe Park's facade. *Familiar. Home.*

But as he drew closer, his eye caught on a black wreath hanging in place of the knocker against the stark white of the front door.

Grandmother?

He ran the last few yards to the door, regret pounding in his ears.

Too late.

Too late to prove to his grandmother that he could make something worthwhile of his life. That he finally understood what she'd tried to impress upon him, all those years ago when he'd been too shrouded in anger and resentment to hear: what it truly meant to be a gentleman of worth.

His hand yanked against the portmanteau strap, the leather biting into his palm. No stopping here, then. He'd better have stayed on the coach to London.

He touched his free hand against the two square columns flanking the left of the door, one after the other, in silent tribute to his grandmother. She'd always insisted it would bring good luck, placing a palm on each.

Spencer jerked when, without warning, Beechcombe's front door creaked open. "Lord Stiles. We did not think to see you so soon," an older man in livery said.

A passing breeze caught at a black ribbon on the mourning wreath, sending it tickling against Spencer's cheek. "Not soon enough," he muttered.

The footman's forehead wrinkled. "My lord?"

Spencer gestured to the wreath. "My grandmother. She is gone?"

"I'm sorry, my lord," the man said, regret carving lines in his face. "Quite sudden, it was, though Mrs. Frith says she did not suffer at the end. The burial took place a week ago Friday."

Spencer ground his teeth against the sudden rush of feeling. "At the parish churchyard?"

"Yes, my lord. Although the stonemason is still working on the engraving."

"Who commissioned it? My wi—"

He stopped, his tongue tripping over the unaccustomed word.

"Lady Stiles?" the footman finally asked, papering over the awkward silence. "No, I believe your father made the arrangements."

Yes, to be sure he had. How silly to have even asked.

Spencer took a deep breath. "Lord Morse is still here, then? At Beechcombe?"

The footman shook his head. "No, he returned to town immediately after the funeral. Parliament is still in session, you see."

"Did my—did Lady Stiles accompany him? Or did she return with her father to Birmingham?"

"No, my lord. Lady Stiles remains in residence."

"Here? By herself?" Spencer swore. Not quite under his breath, if the footman's widening eyes were any indication.

But what right did he have to be upset? If he, her husband, had not cared enough to stay with Philadelphia, to offer her his protection, why should he expect that anyone else would?

"You will find her in the library, I believe," the footman said. "Shall I take your valise, my lord?"

If his wife was at Beechcombe, then he'd have to hold off

going on to London. His innards roiled in a distinctly unpleasant fashion. He hadn't expected to encounter her so soon, the person whom he'd most wronged.

But perhaps it was for the best. The sooner he faced Philadelphia, and then his father, the sooner he could begin to rehabilitate his reputation among the *ton*. Spencer nodded as he handed over his valise, then strode down the hall toward the back of the house.

After the hard wooden planks and dirt floors of the buildings in Sierra Leone, the plush carpet of the passageway felt odd under his boots. And so quiet, too!

His grandmother had never been a great reader, but she'd loved to sit in Beechcombe Park's library, gazing up at the dolphins, sea nymphs, and anchors on the ornate plasterwork ceiling that her father, an admiral, had commissioned. Had she taught the sickly slip of a girl Spencer had married to appreciate them too?

He pushed wide the half-open library door, wondering how his wife might have changed in the years they had been apart. But the only woman in the room was a maidservant. Humming an unfamiliar ditty and absorbed in her dusting, she'd taken no notice of the opening of the door, or of the squeaking of his boots. A curl of tawny-brown hair had escaped from the monstrosity of a mobcap she wore; an apron covered a slim but shapely figure, its pert bosom lifting as she reached for a book on a high shelf.

An unexpected barb of lust rooted him to the spot. What in hell?

He'd almost forgotten, it had been so long since he'd felt anything so strong. Not in all his years in Africa, not during the weeks right before he'd left England, either, when he'd thought he'd never feel anything again. A fitting punishment for his sins, he'd thought then, that enjoyment of pleasures of the flesh seemed to have been taken entirely from him.

After that first year in Sierra Leone, when the worst of his grief and guilt had begun to wane and desire once again began to stir, Spencer might have invited a woman to his bed. No European in Freetown looked askance at a white man lying with a Black woman, or employing one as mistress. Some contemptible beasts even bragged about taking them whether they would or no. Spencer eschewed such company, and chose to slake to his sexual appetites alone, wanting to be a better man, a better husband, even in absentia.

Spencer shivered, then gave himself a short, sharp shake. Even if his interactions with women had been few and far between since he'd left England, lusting after the servants was decidedly *not* the way to show he'd turned over a new, more worthy leaf.

He cleared his throat, not wishing to startle the chit. "Where might I find Lady Stiles?"

The girl—no, woman, he saw now as she jerked to face him —opened her mouth, but no words came out. In her pale face, her eyes, blue as a canary damselfish, fixed on him, unblinking.

A man could lose his soul in such eyes.

"Stiles?" she whispered as the duster dropped from her hand.

He frowned. "*Lord* Stiles, yes. You are employed here?"

"Employed?" The woman laughed, a sharp, disquieting sound.

Had his grandmother taken pity and employed a servant not altogether right in the mind? He took another step into the room. "Come now, girl, answer the question."

Damn, but his voice sounded harsh! It wasn't the poor thing's fault he found himself inappropriately drawn to her. And he'd given his word to Mr. Hoffmann that he'd stop taking out his anger at himself on others.

He drew in a deep breath. "Would you tell me where I might find Lady Stiles?"

"Lady Stiles?" At this laugh, even more unsettling than the first, something urged him to flee. But he could not. For something else, something strangely fascinated by the odd creature, compelled him to step closer.

"Do you not recognize me, my lord?" she asked. "Not even after having had me in your bed?"

In his bed? He jerked down the hand that had risen without his bidding to reach for her. Lord, was she a fey spirit who could somehow read his mind?

But no, those blushing cheeks, those suddenly snapping blue eyes—they belonged to no spirit, no ghost. And those few short words—they hadn't been spoken in the tones of a servant, had they?

His eyes fixed on his grandmother's chatelaine, hanging from her skirt.

"Who are you?" he asked, even as shocking tendrils of recognition began to twine about his brain.

The woman stared at him for a few long moments, agitation in every line of her long, graceful neck, in the pulse that bounded so rapidly at its base. Then, to his shock, she yanked off that ugly cap, pulled free of the dusty apron, and then sank into a curtsey worthy of the finest lady making her debut before the queen.

"Philadelphia Burnett, my lord," she said. "Or, if you prefer the formalities, Viscountess Stiles. Your wife."